DUEL TO THE DEATH!

He was huge, a monster who had killed countless numbers of men usually with one blow. But Stone was fast—and he wasn't about to fight like the oversized killer. The Last Ranger had his own nasty style—one called survival. He danced around the gang topman. Again and again his knife ripped into flesh and then pulled out... Vorstel staggered backward and slammed hard into the wall, cracking the back of his head—though it hardly mattered anymore...

Then Stone heard a sudden sound and whipped around holding the knife at ready. But he was too late—Rudolph was there—right in his face—the huge knife with its cracked bond handle coming in like an ICBM from hell. In a fraction of an instant, Stone knew he was a dead man—that he couldn't duck, move, parry or stab the bastard who was just a foot from his nose and coming at him. His whole body tensed up as he prepared to die...

Also By Craig Sargent

The Last Ranger
The Savage Stronghold
The Madman's Mansion
The Rabid Brigadier
The War Weapons
The Warlord's Revenge

Published by
POPULAR LIBRARY

THE VILE VILLAGE

CRAIG SARGENT

POPULAR LIBRARY

An Imprint of Warner Books, Inc.

A Warner Communications Company

POPULAR LIBRARY EDITION

Popular Library ® and the fanciful P design are registered
trademarks of Warner Books, Inc.

Popular Library books are published by
Warner Books, Inc.
666 Fifth Avenue
New York, N.Y. 10103

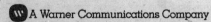 A Warner Communications Company

Printed in the United States of America

First Printing: April, 1988

10 9 8 7 6 5 4 3 2 1

Chapter One _____

_____

The first drop of burning rain hit a falcon flying about a hundred feet up. The bird of prey had been in storms before—many times. Its feathers easily insulated it from any but the worst and most drenching of rains. Thus it stayed aloft, ignoring the thick drops that fell that day. It had to eat, find food. For some reason hunting had been very hard the last few weeks. The falcon didn't know why. Such were not the thoughts of a hawk—to question time or cause and effect. But it did feel a gnawing sensation in its guts that grew stronger with every hour. So it hunted, searching for the prey it lived on—rabbits, moles, a lizard or two. It swung around in wide, lazy circles, more like a kite than a living bird, for it barely moved its wings or expended any muscular energy, so precise was its ability to use the thermals and currents that filled the air everywhere in complex waves invisible to all but itself.

A second drop, and a third one fell. Soon the air was filled with the water, huge drops the size of marbles, falling from the dark clouds above. Then the falcon felt something else, stronger even than the hunger biting at its stomach: a burning sensation along its wings and body. It tried to fly faster to get away from the pain. But that only seemed to increase the electric sensation. It had felt pain before—had been stung by a wasp, had come in hard against its mountain nest and poked a branch through its wing. But these had been brief, sharp pains, ones that vanished quickly and healed.

This was a new pain, a sensation unlike anything the falcon had ever experienced before. It was burning everywhere along its body now—fibers of pure fire that sent shock waves through the falcon's entire sensory apparatus. And suddenly the falcon knew it was in trouble, big trouble. It started to head down to find cover but discovered that it could hardly use its wings. They, too, felt like they were on fire. The bird of prey began jerking wildly, its wings vibrating on each side of it in muscle spasms. Then the falcon's whole body went haywire, twisting and flipping around in the air like some sort of rabid creature having a fit.

It spun down from the sky without a bit of the breathtaking grace it had once possessed, and slammed into a field of small boulders, smashing itself instantly to a bloody pulp on the granite surface. The mess that was left of it seemed to send up a white smoke from every cell of its pulverized body. And as the rains continued to fall in a deluge, the steaming pile was quickly washed down the side of the boulder. In seconds there was nothing left of the falcon, not a single clue that it had ever lived.

Martin Stone looked up at the storm clouds gathering above him and shivered a little deeper in his soul. He knew they were heading straight for him. Mountainous thunderheads filling the heavens like an ocean of writhing whales, twisting and grinding around one another as they descended eagerly toward the dry earth below. Had it been normal rain, rain of the old days, Stone would have enjoyed the drenching. There was nothing like riding along on a 1200-cc Harley Davidson through the pouring drops that had, in the past, been more exhilarating.

But these clouds were different. Even though they were still relatively high, Stone could see the pulsing patterns of energy in their cores. The damn things were like furnaces. Black as soot around the edges, then gray toward the belly —but with streaks of red and purple running through them everywhere like a system of veins. The clouds throbbed with luminescence, pulsing alternately dark and then light every few seconds. Stone knew that the clouds were radioactive— and that they had come to claim a shitload of living souls.

As if in telepathic agreement, a loud whine went up just behind him on the backseat of the Harley Electraglide he was driving down a rutted backcountry road in southwestern Colorado. A furred shape put its front paws up on Stone's shoulders and made a quite ungodly noise into its master's right ear, as if auditioning for lead singer in a punk-rock band.

"Jesus fucking Christ, dog, keep the decibel level down, okay? A deaf master is not a good provider." Stone pulled his head away sharply to the side without easing his hand from the handle of his Harley as he moved down the increasingly dark dirt road. The pitbull suddenly lost its footing on his shoulder as Stone moved—and started falling forward fast, heading off the bike and toward the ground. Only the fighting terrier's super-fast reflexes enabled it to throw its front paw forward onto the seat and twist its body back to the side, stopping itself at the last second. But its face slammed hard into Stone's gun butt, which protruded from his hip, and the canine let out a howl of displeasure. At last the animal got itself straightened out and clamped both pairs of legs hard around the black leather seat. Its heart was beating like a jackhammer from the near fall at thirty-plus miles per hour onto the rocky road.

Stone searched ahead for cover but didn't see a hell of a lot that looked promising. He was in low foothills covered with mostly scraggly-looking firs—not much protection. Stone knew that the clouds and the rains they would release were highly poisoned with radioactivity. He had been fleeing the damn fallout for days now, staying just ahead of it. But it had caught up as it swept south and west—the remnants of an atomic bomb that had been detonated just days before. It had been aimed at him but had killed the man who had fired it, General Patton III, a madman who had been plotting to exterminate select groups and races around America. Still, it all hardly mattered now. For the fallout, the high-rad clouds that had swept off around the countryside all over Colorado and Utah, was not prejudiced in any way. It would kill anyone it could, regardless of race, creed, color, religion, or species.

He came to an intersection of four roads and brought the bike to a complete stop, setting the Harley into neutral. Stone pulled out a half-torn map and stared down at it through the darkening twilight. He couldn't find the junction on it at all. But then, these were backcountry dirt lanes and probably never had made it to official registries—when there had been such things. His compass didn't seem to be worth shit, Stone saw for the twentieth time that week. The rad clouds were affecting the magnetism of the area as well, making the needle of his bike's built-in compass spin around and around like a roulette wheel unable to stop itself.

Stone got off the bike, the auto kickstand snapping down into place, took out a fourteen-inch hunting knife, and held it firmly in his right hand.

"Okay, pal—you tell me," Stone said, not sure if he was addressing the knife, or fate in general. He gripped the stag bone handle and threw it up into the air. The custom bowie spun around about eight times and then came down—the point aiming at the road on the right. Stone picked the knife up, dusted it off against his camouflage pants, and re-mounted the Harley, disgusted to see the pitbull absolutely immobile on the back. Sometimes the dog seemed about the laziest creature on the face of the earth. It was tough—that was for damn sure—but it had definite slothlike tendencies in its character as well.

He threw the 1200-cc into gear, and the bike jumped forward, the bullterrier having to grip extra hard for a second as the gravity started sucking it backward. Stone wheeled the big bike over onto the road on the right, the narrowest of the four, and shot quickly up to about forty miles per hour. He kept glancing nervously over his shoulder, but the damn clouds seemed to be hanging right over his head like immense black vultures, just biding their time until they could swoop down nd peck out his eyes, eat his heart with cloudy beaks. He ould smell the storm clouds in the air now. What they con- ined had a definite stench that was foul and dank, like the nnards of some long dead corpse, something rotting and nfathomably diseased. Even Excaliber, behind him on the eat, let out a loud half snort/half sneeze as he seemed to try to lear his black nostrils of the odor. But there was no getting rid f it; the perfume of infinite rot was blanketing them as the louds dropped ever lower, as if trying to touch the hair on heir heads.

The sky seemed to grow first greenish, like the cheeks of a cadaver—and then dark, very dark. It took hardly more than hirty seconds for it to go from a dim but seeable twilight to a hurricane black, as if the vanishing sun had been ripped from the sky and swallowed whole by the advancing army of clouds. Stone switched on the headlight of the Harley, and it cut a band of yellowish-white illumination through the black- and-gray mists of the road ahead, the air itself so thick with moisture that it was as if he were looking through a diffracting prism as the water molecules in the air bent the images around him, making everything shimmer and waver like a mirage in the desert. Stone had to keep blinking his eyes, squinting hard to make sure he could even see where the hell he was going. It was like driving into a dream—or a nightmare.

Before he even had a chance to pull off the road and get under one of the junkie-thin trees that lined it, the black thunderheads, less than a thousand yards above him, let out a massive, thunderous explosion so that the whole sky filled with crackling lightning bolts that spiderwebbed off in every direction, streaks of fire slamming into the earth all around him. Then the great mountain of moisture opened up as if a dam had burst, and instantaneously Stone couldn't see an inch ahead of him as sheets of water completely covered his face and eyes.

He heard squeals of pain from behind him, and before he could tell the damn dog to shut up, Stone knew why. The rain burned! Burned like a motherfucker! Already, on his face and hands, and he could feel it as it soaked through his

leather jacket and the thick camouflage fatigues on his legs.
At first it stung almost like a wasp or a bee sting. But within
seconds, as it penetrated his epidermis and made contact
with nerve cells, Stone let out a yowl of pain of his own.
The stuff felt like fire, like what he had imagined napalm
would feel like—he had seen pictures of people running
with the stuff burning all over them. Water was supposed to
be wet. But this fucking stuff burned up and down his exposed flesh like waves of flame—of the real stuff.

Suddenly Stone couldn't see at all, and his eyes seemed to
explode in agony, as if razor blades were being dragged
across them. He tried to stop, but he was steering blind.
There was a loud crunching sound as the Harley slammed
into a tree, and then he and the dog were flying through the
rain-soaked air. They both came down hard on the road
about thirty feet ahead, a few yards apart. The pitbull
howled from the sharp pain of the burning drops permeating
its hide—already little pits of burned hair were appearing
here and there, the pelt all red and raised. Stone found himself facedown in the stinking mud and tried to rise. But he
couldn't. Everything burned horribly. And before he knew
it, as his mind reeled from the burning flood, he was joining
the pitbull in its animal screams of fear.

But within agonizing seconds the pain was too much for
both of their overloaded nervous systems to handle. Like
fuses blowing in the basement, their brains both clicked into
darkness. And as the storm continued to howl overhead,
sending reservoirs of radioactive water down over them and
the surrounding land, both creatures—human and canine—
fell into a merciful sleep. And as they slept in a total, wet
blackness, their skin sent up little puffs of acrid white smoke
wherever the rain touched it.

Chapter
Two

"**U**gh, it's uglier than you are," a teenage boy, not older than fifteen, yelled as he ran along waving something burned and hideous in his hand.

"Is not, is not," his younger and fatter companion screamed out, running as fast as his thick, stumpy legs could carry him, trying to get away from the blackened mass of what had once been a deer's head but now resembled nothing more than something that might have been found in the aftermath of Hiroshima or Nagasaki—a swollen, misshapen, charred mass of melted teeth, and eyeballs that had turned to coal, twisting like snails halfway out of their socket homes.

The older teen, dressed in jeans, a tattered shirt, and not a thing on his feet, kept running circles around the fatter, shorter one, as he was so much faster. He poked the still steaming mess at the boy, waving it into his face.

"Eat it, eat it—Chester eats it. Eats dead slime. Swallows it all the time."

"Fuck you, fuck yooouuuuu," the fat one screamed, waving at the air with his pudgy hands like windshield wipers on overdrive. Totally frustrated at being unable to escape from his older brother and getting a piece of the hot slime right on his nose, Chester sank to his knees, put his arms over his head, and burst into tears.

Ponzo, his brother, older by three years and taller by six inches, laughed for a few more seconds, wanting to squeeze all the sadistic glee he could from the situation. Then he threw the oily, burned head away so it landed in some thorn-bushes and sent out a gush of ooze where the barbs pierced its barbecued flesh.

"All right, all right, you fat sissy—I dumped it, okay?" Ponzo said, standing over Chester and opening his arms wide to show he had nothing to inflict psychic torture with. Chester sniffled, peeked through his fingers, and seeing that Ponzo had given up, rose, wiping his reddened nose.

"Ahh," Ponzo screamed, whipping his right hand around fast and squashing it against Chester's face. The molten eye-ball of the radioactively poached deer crushed all over the ten-year-old's cheek and slid down the side in a paste of black and pink.

"You bastard, you. You bastard," Chester screamed, wip-ing frantically at the offending substance with the sleeves of his long-sleeve plaid shirt. He got most of it, but some stuck to him like burned jelly and left a sickening smell like a piece of burger left out in the summer sun for about a week. He reached for a little piece of it on the ground to throw back at his brother, but Ponzo was already running off, laughing as the fat one followed behind, lumbering along like an out-of-shape cow.

The two boys had been finding all sorts of disgusting ob-jects as they ran through the fields near their home, a sprawling farm some four miles off. The rains of the night before had decimated about a five-mile-wide swath of land for hundreds of miles. And in its midst—though the boys had no idea what had caused the devastation—they found smoking heaps of things left in melted piles everywhere, the leaves and cones burned off trees as if they had been sprayed with a blowtorch.

They didn't know what had caused it, but they sure as hell

could see the results. Their bare feet would have felt the high-rad moisture that still remained on the ground, in the soil, for it was hot like beach sand, except that the soles of both their feet were extremely tough, as neither of them had ever worn shoes. So they ran along, poking and prodding the nightmarish remains of all that they passed—raccoons burned down to smoking dust mops, elk with blackened horns set on burned-out husks of bodies, like things that had been dissolved by acid. Both boys had already seen some pretty nasty things in their short lives, but this was by far the worst.

"Hey, look here," Ponzo suddenly screamed from over a rise as the fat one lumbered up behind him, pressing his hands against his knees with each grunting step to get him up.

"It's a man—and a dog," Chester said breathlessly as he reached Ponzo's side.

"Of course it's a man and a dog. What are you, an idiot or something? Jesus, Chester—I don't know about you." He poked at the man whose face and arms appeared to be broken out in boils, the skin itself reddened and blistered in numerous places. Ponzo poked the tip of a branch in the thing's stomach, then in its face. He was sure it was dead until the tip suddenly entered the prone figure's nose for a second. There was an explosive roar as the man sneezed violently, his head jerking up out of the mud for an instant and then slamming down again.

As surely as if a corpse had risen from the grave—or a ghost had walked through a tree—the two youths ran screaming in terror from the event, sure that the thing was some sort of ghoul coming to get them. But after racing nearly a quarter of a mile and discovering that nothing was in fact pursuing them, Ponzo, his curiosity getting the better of him, turned and started back. Chester followed reluctantly, being more afraid of being trapped alone out in these woods with their dog packs—and other things—than having to return to the sneezing corpse.

But if the puffed-up man lying in the dirt had any intentions of going after the two boys, he hadn't tried too hard. In fact, he hadn't moved an inch, Ponzo saw as he came back. The man and dog might be alive—but not for long. Ponzo bent down and examined the dog. Even though there were little burned holes right in its fur, oozing craters here and there where the high-rad rain had penetrated into the pelt, even though it was horribly messed up, he could see that the animal was, or at least had been, beautiful. He stroked the dog softly under the neck, and it opened one eye slightly, barely able to move even the eyelid. The disarmingly intelligent eyes of the pitbull caught the youth full in the face, and in a flash he felt the power of the animal and knew he couldn't let these two die. People he could do without—but dogs he had always loved. There were four back at the farm, big strapping things that could make mincemeat out of this one. On the spot he decided to try to help them.

"Let's strip him," the fat boy said, rubbing his hands together and getting down on one knee as he reached into the man's jacket, searching for booty.

"Get your damn hand outa there before I takes it off," the older boy said, slapping hard at the offending appendage with a small branch, like a schoolmarm slapping an errant student with a ruler. "You really are a pig, aren't you? Jesus, Chester," his brother said, shaking his head.

"Well, why not—we found 'em. It's the scavenger's law, you know—what you find you keep. It's the law of the land, Ponzo."

"You know what Dad, what Undertaker said," Ponzo replied with disgust, herding the fat boy away from the body by whipping him quickly but not very hard on the shoulder like a cowboy heading a steer back into line. "You can strip the dead—but not the living. You go to hell for doing that Chester. Hell."

"Well, how the hell *we* going to help them?" the fat boy asked, suddenly having a horrified image in his head of having to somehow carry the man on his back, which he knew would kill him long before they had gone the three or four miles back to the farmhouse.

"We'll—we'll—" Ponzo said, looking around. "There—the motorcycle—we'll put them on that."

"But you don't know how to drive," Chester said, taunting the boy, as it was a sore point with their father, who hadn't permitted Ponzo to drive the family tractor yet, saying he was too irresponsible.

"So we'll roll the stupid thing, you idiot," Ponzo said, leaning over and slapping the boy on the back of the head to make him stop his whining.

Ten minutes later they had somehow righted the big Harley and lifted the two weak, groaning bodies onto the seat, draping them over the top like animal carcasses brought back from the hunt. Both boys were quite strong—even Chester, with his layers of fat from eating too much fresh farm cooking. But they had spent their lives working their asses off in the many chores of farm life and had muscles that ran deep. Walking along one on each side, holding tight onto the handlebars of the Harley, they wheeled the vehicle forward.

It was tough going at first, as Chester kept somehow losing the grip on his bar and the whole thing would shift to the right, threatening to topple over. But they went slowly and after several minutes got the hang of it. They didn't exactly hit cruising speed, but the two were able to get up to a respectable five miles per hour or so as they headed up and down the fields of wildflowers, purple and red and white and blue in their resplendent brilliance. Going downhill was the easy part—uphill the hard. Chester was particularly worried about the final rise just before the farm. And he was right to be, for they had hardly reached the top when he slipped in some hogshit along the side of a path and went down hard. The whole bike tilted over, and the unconscious occupants were thrown to the ground where they rolled around a little and came to a stop.

It took the boys another ten minutes to get the whole damn thing straightened out and their wards all loaded up again. This time they got the bike to the top of the hill first. But from then on it was all downhill and easy sailing across

the half mile to the main house. There were neighings and
barks, slurpings and caws of countless domesticated animals. There were pens of pigs and chickens, and many dogs
were running around the place. As the two teens got closer,
they saw that there was a lot of activity in the main open
yard in between two red silo-topped barns. About twenty
people—from young children not older than four to old,
wrinkled women in their eighties—all were sawing, sand-
ing, pounding, and nailing pieces of wood together, making
coffins.

"What the hell you got there?" a young face screamed out,
looking up from the nail he was pounding into some jag-
gedly sawed pine planking. A dozen other faces also swung
up and around, and for a few moments there was a sudden,
complete cessation of sound as the entire crew stared at what
the cats had dragged home. There was a certain similarity to
many of the faces—a similar slant of brow, placing of eyes,
shape of nose. Which was hardly surprising, as the gathering
was basically one huge extended family—the Hanson family, run by the patriarch, grandfather, and sire of half those
present—Bradley "Undertaker" Hanson, who stood over the
coffin watching it all with a stern eye.

"Found this bunch out by the gorge," Ponzo yelled back,
beaming with pride at his find, as was his brother, Chester,
who knew that something like this would be worth a mini-
mum of a few extra desserts—and the maximum of a knife
or some object of value. Undertaker liked to run things like a
general, rewarding those who were "clever" and punishing
those who were "stupid."

"Back to work, all of you," he shouted to the box makers.
"Keep your eyes on the damn nails—there's money to be
made tonight. Five were killed this afternoon in town.
Five . . ." His eyes lit up with a certain glee at the presence
of the Grim Reaper. For it meant two dollars a box. Two
times five equals ten. Ten bucks—that was two more horses
for his stable. He patted himself on the back for the thou-
sandth time for starting up the undertaking business as his

second vocation—after he had seen many years before that farming alone wouldn't support him. Not with *his* appetites, *his* virility, *his* progeny. With the additional good luck to live just a few miles from one of the bloodiest towns around—Cotopaxi—where they brought the bodies out of the bars and the whorehouses by the wheelbarrow full—he had it made.

In fact, "Others' tragedies—our blessing," was just one of the Undertaker's many expressions, which he quoted sternly to the rest of them.

"They dead?" Undertaker asked, starting forward, his large girth rolling around him as he moved. The man was only about 5'8" tall but must have weighed perhaps 400 pounds. The good life had been good to him, that was for damn sure. Where others had starved, he had prospered. His completely bald head and red-cheeked face, sitting atop the ovular body below, created nothing so much as the impression of two eggs atop one another—one immense, the other the size of a bowling ball, both of them sort of rotating around each other like two planets in orbit as he walked along.

"Hmm," Undertaker said with interest as he saw the value of the motorcycle. He had an old one in the shed, but it was rusted, barely functional. This one, on the other hand, was in perfect order and had the added feature of weapons. He leaned down as his two sons—both like all the male children, bald as M&M's—held the heavy bike a little unsteadily. Chester, in particular, was exhausted from the afternoon's exertions. Undertaker got down on one knee with a *whoomph* of expelled air and looked into Stone's face, which was hanging down over one side of the leather seat. He couldn't see any noticeable sign of breathing but could see the horrendous red boils and bumps all over the man's face and neck. Undertaker knew what it was instantly. His years of undertaking work, and the reading of a number of medical journals, had actually made him quite a competent doctor capable of treating his own family—more than one member of which he had saved by his diagnoses.

Radiation poisoning! The man had been exposed to some powerful radioactive source—perhaps the rains that had just missed the farm the night before. The patriarch reached out, grabbed hold of Stone's nose, and tweaked it hard. The figure let out a little sharp sound, and the head tried to stir, the eyes opening for a split second and then closing again as the fever-racked body let its head fall back to the metal side of the motorcycle.

"Still ticking, huh, mister?" Undertaker said with a laugh, slapping the unconscious Stone on the shoulder. He turned to the left and did a similar test to the dog, which lay there equally limp. The nose of a dog being the most sensitive spot by far on its body, the pitbull suddenly opened both eyes and somehow found the energy to snap up hard at whatever was fucking with its snout. Then it collapsed back again, as Undertaker Hanson nearly fell backward from the sudden "attack."

"Damn thing has some spunk in it, I'll tell you that, Undertaker said with a harsh laugh as he rose slowly to both feet and dusted himself off.

"Chester said we should strip 'em," Ponzo said, looking over accusingly at his brother.

"Did not, did not," Chester screamed back, nearly letting the bike fall over in his anger.

"Oh, shut up, you moron," Undertaker snapped, suddenly pulling a long piece of hickory from his sleeve and whopping the lad right on the top of his bald head. The youth's eyes rolled around in his face like rotted fruits in a slot machine—and he shut up.

"I tol' you once, I tol' you a thousand times," Undertaker said sternly. "If they's dead, you can strip 'em. 'Cause the dead don't need what they got. But if they's living, then you gotta treat 'em like a man. Otherwise you'll go to hell."

"But how can you treat a dog like a man?" Chester asked dumbly, his lower jaw hanging open.

"How can one of my own kin have no brain at all?" Undertaker asked with an exasperated roar as he stared at the youngest of his sons—to his thinking the worst of the lot. "Now come on," he said sharply. "Take 'em up to the attic, get Katie and LuAnn to get set up, and then get your damn asses down here, 'cause we got coffins to build—goddamn coffins to build. It's honey time. It's raining corpses."

Chapter Three _____

M artin Stone floated between life and death. It was a strange sensation, sort of like being a child floating in a bathtub, or on a rubber mattress at the beach —when there had been such things—bobbing up and down in the waves. He floated between this world and something else. Something he couldn't see clearly but could feel, feel pulling him with a magnetic intensity, as if it wanted him real bad.

When he floated back to this world—to the earth world, the world of solid things that lived and breathed—he felt pain, such intense pain as he had never experienced before. He didn't know what was wrong with him. He had hardly enough rationality left in his fevered brain to think it all through. He was just an animal in this world, burning up with tongues of fire coursing through every cell. He had been hurt, whoever "he" was. Hurt real bad.

When he drifted back to the other world—through a tunnel of diamonds all rippling blue and white like they were made of star material—things were more insubstantial. There were beings there—strange beings, both frightening and beautiful—all of them hard to see, as if he were looking through an unfathomably deep, shadow-filled ocean. They floated in the luminescent haze that surrounded them. And they were calling to him. Calling for him to join them: "Stone, Martin Stone. Life is no longer for you. This is your new state. Come . . . come . . . come!

"Martin Stone, it is so beautiful here. Do not resist. Death is . . . love."

Then there were other voices around him pulling him back from the insubstantial world. But these were not so angelic, and seductive. They were yelling at him. Harsh lights suddenly filled his eyes, and he felt his physical being being moved around, shifted, things poked into it and put on it. Though, again, just who or what that body was, was quite beyond him. His was a primal existence. He was a primitive being in a sea of pain who had intelligence but no past—and no future.

Then he felt himself leaving his body again and shooting through the ceiling of the room he was in. He seemed to turn to some kind of dust that could pass through solid material, could fly right into the heavens like something sucked up in a tornado. Then he was staring down at himself from far up. It was as if he were a hundred miles above his burned, blistered body. And when he saw the damaged flesh—and the canine lying on a bed next to it in similarly fucked-up fashion—suddenly he knew who he was, and that, in fact, although it would be nice to rest for the next billion, trillion years and hang out with the spirit mists that flew around him, he just had too much to do at this exact moment, though he would be glad to say hello to anyone's relatives back on earth.

But the ethereal shapes of indeterminate species had other ideas. Cloaked in a gray mist, they reached for him with arms that rippled with smoke, fingers that clutched with currents of dark electricity, trying to bring him down, trying to drag him off into the goddamn clouds somewhere, like a fucking street mugging in heaven.

Stone had learned to kick ass on earth, and he was damned if he wasn't going to go out without a good fight—

even in heaven or hell. He started clawing and punching his way back through the crowds of the dead. And though it was slow going, he almost began making some headway when suddenly he saw a sight that froze him in his tracks, made his heart—what there was left of it—seem to harden like setting concrete in his chest.

His mother and father—only both were dead, the way they had been when he'd last seen them. His father, all blue in the face and his once crystal eyes flat and dead like balls of mud. His mother was horrible. She had been raped and mutilated in her last moments, and it was as if the crime had just happened and the blood still oozed from her ripped flesh, the hair torn from her skull in bloody clumps.

Both of them reached for him as if welcoming him home after a long vaction.

"Oh, Martin, Martin, you've come," his dead mother said. She came toward him with bleeding fingers outstretched, scraping at him, while his father walked stiff-legged like something from a bad B movie. Stone stood mesmerized, not able to move an inch from the limbo zone he was in. Yet somehow he knew that if they touched him or grabbed him, he would be dead. Would be like *them*. And Martin Stone didn't want to be dead. Didn't want to be like that.

He pushed with all the willpower of his still living spirit, which dangled on the scales as Undertaker's daughters gave Stone's body this pill and that ointment, this antirad liquid, that rubdown with cold mud to bring down his body temperature, which rose to 108° at times. Somehow he broke through the ranks of the dead, sending dark spirits flying like rotting tenpins. He dove from the throbbing black cloud he was in—down, down—as if diving toward the bottom of a swimming pool where a precious jewel lay, the jewel of his body, of himself. The electric hands reached out for him with dark currents, and slime-coated ectoplasmic flesh. But they couldn't reach. And he disappeared back down toward the living, the real, the substantial.

A screaming chorus of anger went up as he slipped from

their fingers, as his soul escaped from their dark land. They reached after him, sending out wispy talons, but these merely evaporated in the air like smoke from a cigarette. For he was gone—heading down like a meteor, out of their grasp, their influence. For now.

Stone felt himself shooting through a tube. He was in the Bobsled at Coney Island. It was great. He twisted and turned as bands of light spun in concentric circles of Day-Glo color around him, as if he were inside a barber's pole. And his father was sitting next to him. His father, the Major, had brought little Martin to New York City—and the world-famous amusement park at Coney Island. And it was so much fun. But now Martin was going faster, too fast, and he reached out for support against the sides of the car. But there was nothing there—only air. And then he was falling terribly fast.

There were sounds above him, and he opened his eyes fractionally, which let in a fire of light that seemed to pierce every optic nerve. Huge, blubbery lips were moving above, but they were speaking in slow motion and he couldn't understand a damn thing they were saying. Then he saw the fat face attached to the lips. Jowled and with shining bald head, Undertaker stared down at him. And Martin Stone knew without question that he had died and gone to hell. And that the devil had hair-loss problems too.

Chapter
Four _____

A tongue was in his eye. It was long and it was wet. And it stroked at his face over and over, like a piece of wet sandpaper trying to plane down his nose and cheeks to the bone. There was the overpowering scent of dog and alcohol and numerous other strong-smelling substances. He felt like he was drowning.

Martin Stone opened one eye to see an immense furred face about one inch from his own. Its right eye was focused intently on his own partially opened eyelids, and it let out a squeal that quickly grew to a shrill and deafening intensity. And Stone knew he was alive—if only because it hurt his ears so much. He reached out with one arm to swat the animal away and realized at the same instant that it was Excaliber, and that he couldn't move a muscle. It felt like his hands were tied down. Stone knew something else, too —that his entire body felt like it had been through an oven, a meat-grinding and tenderizing session, used as a soccer ball in a grudge match and worse.

"Hey, get away from there," a voice suddenly called out, and Stone saw the dog turn and then a hand pushing it down off the bed he lay tied down on.

"You're awake," the same soft voice asked. Stone saw another half-focused shape right above him. Only this face wasn't bald or furry at all. It was beautiful. "That dog been messin' with you since it woke up yesterday morning," the flush-cheeked, blond-haired female said with a little snort of derisive laughter. "How you feelin', mister?" she asked with a smile. Slowly Stone's eyes were coming into focus, and the more he saw, the more he felt like living. He dimly remembered some battle he had had with gray, amorphous things. But as he had returned to the world of the living and the memory was of the dead, it quickly faded from his skull, popping like a bubble even as he reached with his mind to contain it.

"Tara said you was goin' to die," she said, reaching down and stroking his forehead with a cool, wet cloth. It felt good. "But I said no—this man's got guts inside that burned body. I tell you—"

"What—what do you mean, burned?" Stone asked with puffed lips, which trembled as he spoke. Nothing on him felt like it was in very good shape.

"Pa thinks it was the rains that came by five days ago. Burned you and your damn dog, I'll tell you that. You should see yourself, mister—maybe you shouldn't." She giggled. "You got bumps and sores and boils and all kinds of nasty things all over yourself. I been working on you with my own hands." She held up two small, but strong-looking, hands, callused fingers used to working, and hard. "Undertaker let me stay up here with you once he saw you had a real chance, which was mighty nice of him, all things considered—I mean, since it's peak coffin season right now."

Stone's mind reeled with questions that just gave him a jarring headache as little armies of mental porcupines paraded around in a gallop through his brain.

"Am I going—goin' to make it?" Stone managed to stutter out. If he had such a wall-to-wall carpeting of ugly bumps and couldn't move a muscle, it seemed like a logical question.

"Pa—Undertaker—thinks so. And damned if he ain't the

most smart doctor type in these parts. Not a real doctor, of course," she said with a shy smile, which Stone managed to return with his own. She couldn't have been over eighteen or nineteen years old but was in the full bloom of womanhood. Long reddish-blond hair flowed down each shoulder like little waterfalls of fire, and the blush on her cheeks was like the pink tips of a freshly bloomed mountain rose. Her lips were moist, and Stone felt an insane desire to reach up and kiss them hard. Her face was like a mirror for her inner feelings—her very soul reflected in those twinkling eyes, in her constantly changing expression. Somehow, in a world of death, she was incredibly, wonderfully alive.

"Why can't I move?" Stone asked, trying to raise his hand to scratch something that itched fiercely on his stomach.

"Pa's treatment, mister," the farmgirl went on. "Got so many burns all over your skin, it's all red and tight and dry. We been treating it with all kinds of mud baths that Pa mixed up from his secret recipes. Won't even tell *us* what they is. But he said if you moved at all, it would break the skin, rupture it, so's we got you all tied down, mister. Sorry about that. You do look funny, though. Tied down like Gulliver in the land of the Lilliputians. And all naked the way you are —and all covered with white mud with ground-up junk and herbs in it. You look a little like"—she put her hand over her mouth, trying not to laugh, for it was surely impolite to laugh at the radioactively impaired—"an ice-cream cone with sprinkles all over it." She couldn't contain it, and a series of girlish giggles escaped from around her hand.

Stone somehow managed to crane his neck just a little, just enough to see how completely and horribly ridiculous he looked. Like a mud-caked slug all tied down at arms and legs with leather thongs. He didn't know whether to laugh or cry. The sheer conflict of the two emotions sent his mind reeling again, and he fell back down the black pit into which many tumble but from which few emerge.

Chapter Five

Wen next he awoke, the very first thing Stone did was try his arms, which he found to his intense happiness were no longer strapped down. Though he was still naked and on the bed with a thick white goo over every square inch of him, like the Pillsbury Doughboy saturated with icing. It felt sticky and quite wretched, but figuring that these people knew what the hell they were doing or he wouldn't even still be around, Stone didn't try to start madly wiping it off with the sheets that lay sweat-soaked beneath him.

He glanced around the attic room he was in, the thin light of a silvery dawn just starting to streak in through the cracked windows. He could see that he was in a narrow but long room that came to a single joint at the top in an A-frame. Across from him, lying atop a bed without blankets or pillows, was Excaliber, all sprawled out on his back, looking as happy as a goddamn pig in shit. But Stone could see in the slowly brightening morning that the dog was all flea-bitten, with little patches or missing hair all over its coat, its tail swollen to twice its normal size. The mutt looked like it had been through the wringer—and the washer and the dryer—and they had all been set on "Extra Heavy Wash."

"Jesus Christ," Stone muttered, and he could feel that his own lips had swollen to nearly the size of sausages.

"Ah—it lives, it breathes," the same sweet voice that had been the last thing he heard said from a chair in a still darkened corner of the room. "You slept another two days. What'sa matter, mister?" the girl asked, her face bright with a pearly smile as she walked over to him. "Ain't you never slept before you came to the Hanson Farm and Undertaking Palace?"

"As a matter of fact," Stone replied, managing to rise up to his elbows, though the effort sent sharp little jolts of pain all through his arms and stomach, "no. Never. Not before here. I think I like it." He let himself fall backward, then let out a sharp little bark as his whole back seemed to light up like a roman candle of pain. Stone remembered when he had let himself get badly sunburned a few times when he had been a stupid kid. His back had erupted in little water-filled bubbles and had turned beet-red. It had hurt him so much that he had clutched the wet sheets through the night with tears in his eyes. But this was a different level of pain, a hundred times worse. Still, in front of someone with whom he wouldn't have minded being stranded on a desert island, Stone didn't betray a bit of the pain he was feeling, other than a little quiver of his lower lip from time to time.

"Well, enough sleep," she said firmly, leaning over and grabbing hold of his elbow. It felt like her fingers were hot pincers as they dug into him. "Undertaker says if you ain't dead, it's time for you to get up and contribute something to the work here—as he's spent a fortune on you already." She said the words as if quoting him, then giggled. Again Stone was struck by the way her eyes glistened, how her lips moved as she spoke. He could feel himself heading for another fall—perhaps worse than the one he had just taken.

"All right," Stone said weakly, "but you'll have to help me. I feel like a worm that's been in a blender."

"Sure," she said with a shy smile, and reached forward to

help him. Only as Stone started to sit up did he realize again that he was still completely naked and covered by the white paste.

"Wait, I'm sorry—I—" Stone began to stutter, not even sure what the hell it was he was trying to say.

"Don't worry, mister, I been seeing you stark naked for days now. Who you think been coating you with that slop, turning you over to air you out in the breeze—like some ol' mattress. So don't start getting all shy and blushing on me now."

"Yeah, sure," Stone said dumbly, his brain not functioning clearly enough to make or even think of anything clever to say. She helped him into his clothes as Stone walked around, turning a deeper shade of red than he already was. There was something about a woman helping you into your drawers that could rattle a man's whiskers.

At last, with repressed groans by Stone here and *sorrys* by her there whenever she pulled too hard on a piece of clothing or scratched his leg as she poked it through his pant leg, he was dressed. Stone walked stiffly to the dog, trying not to fall down from the rubberiness in his legs and the dizziness that ran through him in waves of nausea. He felt like a rubber band in the sun.

"What's the matter, boy? You don't look too good." Stone said with concern, standing over the disheveled and partially shaven animal, which opened its eyes like the slits of pillboxes and looked at him.

"In fact, you look like shit," Stone went on as he saw all the bumps and lumps that covered the creature, though he knew he didn't look great himself.

"Been giving him basically the same treatment as you," the girl said. "And I must say he was a better patient than you too. You was always groaning and trying to punch me when I had to change your dressings—but him, he would just lie back, get this dumb sorta smile on his face, and wait for me to scratch his belly.

"That's because he's more of a hedonist than me." Stone smirked.

"A what?" she asked, standing on the other side of the feather mattress on top of the bed frame on which the pitbull lay.

"Someone who loves pleasure," Stone answered, scratching the dog behind the ears so that he let out a little squeal of satisfaction.

"Ain't nothing wrong with pleasure," she said, looking Stone directly in the eyes with a bold, unmistakable sexual energy. "Anyway," she went on as he looked away first, his heart starting to beat too fast, sending the blood to his head like the mercury in a thermometer set over a flame. "I think he's going to be all right too. He was up two, three days ago—but he ate so damn much as soon as we fed him that his stomach got distended and he's been bedridden for two more days now. We're not even going to let the sucker eat next time."

"Good idea," Stone said, looking down at the dog, which would eat itself right into death like a goldfish if it could.

"Goldfish," Stone muttered under his breath as he patted the still bloated guts of the animal hanging down like the pig-stuffed stomach of an anaconda. The animal made a dreadful sound, like a burp, yawn, and howl all at once, and Stone pulled his palm away from the creature's white-furred belly.

"Let's go," the girl said as she came around to Stone's side and took him by the arm. "They'll all be eatin' downstairs—be a good time to meet the whole crew if you can stand it. What's your name?" she asked suddenly. "I been rubbin' you down naked, but I don't even know what the world calls you." She laughed, and again Stone couldn't help but notice how her teeth sparkled like pearls in the golden rays of the half-risen sun.

"I'm Stone," he said. "Martin Stone. And this here's my dog—well, he's not really my dog, but he's chosen to travel with me for the moment. The name he answers to is Excaliber."

"Name's LuAnn, but they all call's me Lou, on account of

I look like my dead brother, Louis." She helped him to the door, supporting him on one shoulder, as she could see that he was having a bit of trouble walking, though she knew he would never admit it.

They'd hardly reached the second-floor landing when Stone could hear them—voices, lots of them. By the time they got to the first floor, to the back, and through the swinging doors into the huge kitchen, it became deafening. There must have been thirty people—from little babies suckling at their mother's breast to eighty-year-old, shriveled-up biddies with toothless mouths sucking on spoons with cereal in them. All of them were eating breakfast as huge buckets of steaming porridge were carried over on long poles and set down atop one of three long wooden tables that filled the ramshackle space, thick with the scents and steam of the foods and the odors of farmers who hadn't taken too many baths recently.

They turned as one as Stone came through the swinging oak doors—and they laughed, a great, thunderous sound that Stone wouldn't forget until his last day. And they pointed at him.

"You look like a snowman who got covered with icing," one of the dirty faces with unkempt hair screamed above the din of human ridicule and canine barking.

"Oh, shut up, all of you!" a bald, fat man screamed out from the head of the biggest table as he reached out with a long hickory stick he had hidden in his sleeve and began bouncing it off the nearest heads with sharp little snaps.

"Now get back to your food—and be happy you got any," the man shouted out, pounding his meaty fist on the table so that all the bowls filled with gruel danced up an inch or two and came down hard, jiggling their contents in little splashes onto the tabletop. "'Cause you got work to do—and 'cause this man is our guest and will be treated accordingly."

The place seemed to quiet down—for a few seconds, anyway—though all eyes remained on Stone even as the mouths below them continued to chew ravenously at the cereal in their bowls. The place reminded Stone of the movie

Oliver Twist, which he'd seen years before. The general
slovenliness of the kitchen and the filthy appearance of the
people in it—ripped shirts and pants, the shoelessness of
most of those present, the gap-toothed smiles—all brought
to mind nothing less than Fagin's pickpocket gang of little
thieves who he had trained to rob and swindle. But aside
from the appearance of things, everyone seemed to be relatively happy and well fed. It was a hell of a lot better than
most of the hovels Stone had seen in his travels around the
cesspool that was now America.

"Here, come sit here," the bald face bellowed, and
LuAnn led Stone over to the table, helping him right to
the long bench seat, where he plopped down hard when
she let go.

"Ah, you look like hell," the ruddy face said. "But you'll
live. Believe me, I know—I've seen a lot of 'em go out that
way. You'd be dead already, my friend, if it was your time."

"Well, that's good to know," Stone intoned without much
energy. He felt like he hardly existed, like he was hardly
more substantial than the creatures he had been battling with
the nights before. While those around him seemed incredibly, painfully alive as they laughed and ate and banged their
forks on the tables, as they hit one another and played dumb
children's games. "But I sure as hell feel dead."

"Food, man—you need food. Look at me," Hanson said
with pride. He slapped his great girth, and every part of him
sort of jiggled around like too much taffy on the end of a
stick. "I eat my fill, and I never get sick. Plague—radiation,
it can't get through a filled stomach. Dammit" he shouted
again, sounding like an elephant horn cutting through the
mayhem of the kitchen. "When a man needs food, goddamn
it, he'd better get food." Three pairs of children had been
carrying the pots back and forth from the roaring hearth that
took up one whole end of the kitchen. They rushed even
faster, trying to keep up with the insatiable demands of the
birdlike mouths that kept opening and snapping shut, gulp-
ing down everything that they carried over.

"Name's Hanson. Bradley "Undertaker" Hanson. I'm

farmer, undertaker, preacher, doctor. You name it, I can do it, or it can't be done. Pleased to meet you, boy. What's your name?"

"Stone," he replied, taking a bite of the steaming oatmeal that sat on the table in front of him, which sent up a mouth-watering funnel of sugary wheat flavor. "Martin Stone. And I sure as hell want to thank you for saving my damn ass. My dog too. Not too many men would have done that. Not from what I've seen out there."

"Well, I ain't like no other man you're likely to meet, and you can bet your aunt's balls on that." The man laughed. A dog suddenly got hold of a piece of meat on the far side of the room, which resulted in quite a commotion, with food flying and animals leaping across tables. But apparently it was a fairly common occurrence, for though Stone looked up, startled, the rest hardly paid it any mind at all.

Suddenly Undertaker leapt up and snapped out his hickory, hitting one of the youngsters at the table about six feet away. The blond, buck-toothed lad jumped straight up in the air with a scream, as if he'd been goosed with an electric prod. A butter knife clanked down onto the table from one of his sleeves.

"Bastard son," Undertaker shouted, his face growing red with an apoplectic rage. "You steal from your own father?"

"I'm s-sorry Pa," the lad stuttered as he stood at rigid attention, shaking like a leaf. "I just wanted to have a knife like all my brudders, here." He motioned with his head around the table. "It ain't fair that I got to wait till I'm sixteen. Already got cut up twice by the Bronson boys in town."

"That's *just* why I didn't give you a damn knife. If I *did*, you would have stabbed one of them Bronsons—and now we'd have us a shooting feud going with 'em. Your father knows best, boy. Always remember that." He squinted closely at the lad and scratched his bald head. "Which one are you, anyway? Name, lad, name?" He snapped his finger impatiently, and the teen stuttered again, as if he couldn't quite remember his own name.

"Andy, s-sir," he at last spat out. "In charge of chicken-feed, wheelbarrow oiling, duck herding, compost, dog feeding, nail straightening—"

"All right, all right," Hanson said, waving his hand and slamming his huge frame back down in his seat. "Come see me later, boy, and we'll talk about punishment. I'm still eating my breakfast." The youth sank down and looked terrified as he sat paralyzed at his place, unable to take another bite of the oatmeal.

"I've sired a lot of children," Hanson said, looking proudly at Stone. "Can't remember them all sometimes. You know how it is." Stone nodded appreciatively, as if he had exactly the same problem. "Paul, John, Ted, Ed, Fred— who the hell can keep up with it? I just make 'em," he said with a laugh, "I don't keep track of 'em." Stone looked quickly around the room and saw an ungodly number of snot-nosed brats chomping down on breakfast—and quite a number of wives, as well, with newborns attached to them. Could they all be Hanson's? Stone wondered. The man looked to be in his sixties—perhaps even his seventies—but he was still powerful, virile. Although huge, Stone knew that within those folds of fat was great strength, and beneath that bald dome, a high intelligence.

Suddenly there was a great commotion at the front door, another round of dogs yapping and ducks quacking out in the yard in a frenzy of fear. One of the young ones opened up the kitchen door, and a tattered man stood there. He had the face of a wizened old elf, like a piece of leather that had been left in the sun for about fifty years. His features were lost in the deep, dry folds that his dark skin had turned to. He stood only about five feet high and held a large, woven straw basket in his arms.

"Sir, sir, I—I—"

"Well, what the hell is it?" Undertaker yelled. "Speak up, man."

"I was told to show you—show you this." He held the basket harder against him, as it clutching a child to his chest. "But—but—"

"But what?" Again Undertaker slammed his ham-sized fist down on the table, and every bowl on it jumped around like frogs on capsizing lily pads. "Damn it man, speak up, will you? If there's one thing I hate, it's people who can't get their damn words out. What's wrong with this world—is everyone slipping back into Cro-Magnon days where we'll all grunt like gorillas?"

"But you're all eating—b-b-breakfast," the farmer said nervously.

"What the hell does that have to do with it?" Undertaker exclaimed, his face turning red. "I said show us your damn business or I'll be after you with my stick, here." Undertaker started to rise, and the man got a strange, sickly expression, then an equally strange little smile. He looked down, opened the top of the straw basket, and grabbed hold of something inside. Rolling his eyes to the ceiling, as if knowing something quite horrible was about to unfold, he lifted the thing out.

It was a head—a human head—and it had been severed just at the top of the neck so it was nearly round in shape and covered in a sheen of its own blood. Its popping eyes half exploded from their sockets as they slid down the front of the face like larvae searching for a home. Its frozen mouth was still screaming—silently—in the most terrified expression Stone had ever seen. Blood dripped down from beneath the opening of the neck, and drops of it could be heard through the sudden and complete silence in the room as every man, woman, and child stopped chewing and took in the horror.

Then it slipped from the tiny man's hand, the blood on the hair making it slide from his fingers. It hit the ground with a slopping sound, then rolled forward under one of the tables. And the gruel, so to speak, hit the fan.

Chapter Six

The man who had let the head fall from his grip apologized profusely for the mess and commotion he had caused. But Undertaker wouldn't hear a word of it, yelling at his numerous progeny that "They'd damned well better get used to grislier sights than a stinking head in a basket if they had any intentions of carrying along in the family business I've worked so hard to establish." After everyone was properly berated and tapped on the head with the stick, Undertaker led the man to his table from which one of his own was unceremoniously deprived of his chair.

"Sit down, mister, sit down," Undertaker said, motioning with his hand for one of the serving children to bring a cup of the steaming brew he was sipping—not real coffee but brewed from a mix of sassafras, bitter herbs, and some old coffee flavoring that he had picked up a whole barrelful of somewhere along the line. It was important to Hanson that visitors like the coffee, as it was such a rare and unknown treat. It impressed them with his wealth and taste. He peered closely into the man's beady eyes as the wizened farmer took a sip, trying to calm himself down.

"Ah, good—so good," the man said with the thinnest

32

razor of a smile. "So long since I had—" Then he looked down at the basket on his lap and remembered why he was there, and the smile vanished as if it had never existed.

"Ah, mister, it was horrible—the most horrible thing I've ever seen," the man said. "I'm sorry," he whispered, putting the cup back down on the table. "I'm being rude in my fear. My name is Miguel Hernandez—I am a farmer about fifteen miles to the north past the bomb crater. The soil is rich there—richer than many places in the territory. And a man could survive, even raise a family and live a life. Except—except—" He looked down at the basket again and seemed about to burst into tears. "Except for the Strathers brothers. They started making us pay a 'tax' about two years ago. But this tax gets bigger every month now. Last week they told us that we'd have to give even more of what we produce. We have nothing anymore. As it is, we can barely feed ourselves, those of us who work the land, and our children. But the additional kilos of wheat and squash they want—we might as well all hang ourselves. . . ."

He paused, let his head drop for a second, and his face, which in its pure state of misery was exposed for an unguarded moment, made the farmer look a thousand years old, with all the pain of a race contained in his lips and moist eyes.

"So we decided to organize. Or try to." He laughed a bitter sound. "Several dozen of us met in one of the cornfields last night to think of some way we could fight back. But the Strathers gang somehow had found out about the meeting. They were waiting. Four of us at the meeting— their heads were sliced off while the rest of us were made to watch. Right in front of us, and we are a close community linked in blood and marriage. They made them kneel and then slowly—slowly—cut off the heads with handsaws while they held the screaming victims down. It was, it was—" He looked as if he were about to burst into tears again as his whole face sort of contorted up into quite a terrified expression.

"Easy, easy," Undertaker encouraged the man softly as the

rest of the family, who were still in the kitchen, looked on, fascinated and repulsed at the same time.

"So I can't ask you to help us, because what can any man do?" Hernandez forced himself to go on. "There are just too many of them. But we have come to ask you to help us bury our dead. We are poor and have even less now, as the gang of murderers who came last night stripped many of our houses. But we have been able to scrape up some things." He stopped and whistled, and a second small old man appeared at the door, just as sun-beaten and shrunken as the first. He dragged an old mule behind him that looked like it had been born around the time of Jesus, so gray and dusty was its flea-bitten hide. Atop the wretched animal were a fifty-pound bag of corn and five live, skinny chickens all squawking like it was Judgment Day as they fluttered, tied together by the feet, feathers shaking off into the air and down onto the kitchen floor.

"It's all right—it's all right." Undertaker laughed, waving his hand toward the man. "Just tell him to take that stuff out back and unload it. It will be payment enough. Fred—or whatever your damn name is," Undertaker bellowed, whipping out his hickory stick at a big red-haired lad who sat in front of the fire eating toast with dripping honey, "get the hell out there and take in those supplies, and tell inventory to get out planking for four"—he looked at the man, who nodded sadly up and down—"four SFs." This was undertaking lingo for "small fries," since from time immemorial undertakers had spoken in code to keep the bereaved from ever really knowing just what the hell they in fact did in a funeral parlor.

"You just go get them bodies back from your cornfield and we'll take care of everything," Undertaker said, slapping the man on the back so he spat out a little mouthful of black coffee. "Tonight—we'll have the funeral tonight, before the wolves come out. They've just been mating and they'll be hungry as hell. The smell of the dead, especially with their heads off and the blood scent drifting over the mountains for miles, will attract a small army of them. Yeah, we gotta work fast Mr. Hernandez."

"We are ready," he said. "My people are just waiting for your okay. The bodies are all packed up and ready to bring to you. We will be back before the sun is down." He took a last sip of the fake coffee, a substance he had once loved— and now hadn't had a sip of in five years. "And thank you, thank you from all my people for this—this kindness. If there is a God in heaven, and I am not sure there is anymore, he will reward you someday for this." With that the man tottered quickly from the room and slammed the wooden door, half hanging on its hinges behind him.

"Come on, you," Undertaker said, addressing Stone loudly so that he thought the big, bald table of a man was about to use the hickory on him as well. But the stick apparently was reserved for immediate family, for he merely rose and started toward the door as Stone somehow dragged his aching, medicine-coated body up and after the man. Undertaker led him out of the house and around to the back as Stone jerkily caught up with him and walked by his side. The sun was warming things now, making Hanson's bald head bead with sweat like a bowling ball covered with wax —and Stone's white coating of medicinal herbs started to dry, harden, and crack all around his body so that he felt like he was some sort of walking mud beast.

"Come on, man, you've used up enough of my precious ointments on that overcooked flesh of yours." Undertaker laughed. "Now make yourself useful around here—help me put some of these coffins together. We've been busy as god-damn beavers for days now. People are dropping like fuck-ing flies."

"Why is it so bad around here?" Stone asked as he hob-bled along behind. "I've seen bad places, but that farmer looked about as scared as they come, like a jackrabbit about to be pancaked by a diesel."

"Ah, it *is* bad around here—you could say that two or three times. One gang of slime would be enough, but no, we have to have two trying to control the same territory. Trying to suck the blood out of the same body twice would be more like it. There's two gangs of murdering swine who between them run things for about a hundred square miles in these parts—the Strathers brothers and the Head Stompers, a local version of the Guardians of Hell. But just as mean and nasty as the original—if not more so. Neither gang has really been able to do the other one in. The Strathers boys are mostly made up of mountain bandits who've hit the big time. They're dumber and not as tough as the bikers, but there are nearly a hundred of them—all armed to the teeth. The Head Stompers, who showed up about a year ago, are as bad as they come. They carry, among other things, razor-sharp scythes they swing around at the ends of long chains. They can come in on their big bikes standing up on the goddamn seats, spinning those things around their heads. I seen 'em once just practicing—it's a sight I wish I could forget. But there are only about three dozen of them. So it's a standoff between the two gangs. A stalemate." He paused.

"But that doesn't go for the people around these parts: the farmers, the townsfolk of Cotopaxi, which serves as headquarters for both bunches of bastards. The place is like a battlefield—so tense, you can cut it with a knife. Everyone —in town and out—is subject to both gang's 'taxes,' and after stealing their money and goods, the gangs force them to spend their remaining pennies in the whorehouses and gin mills of the town to drown their sorrows—and they've got plenty of sorrows to drown. Since the bastards showed up, life has gone from being hard to being a living hell. I'm the only goddamn person making any money around here— other than them. And that's because the murderers always pay their funeral bills. It's a tradition going back to Al Capone. You bumps 'em off, you pays for their little condo in the ground."

As he talked, Undertaker led Stone around to one of the two big red barns. The structure had obviously been used at one time for agricultural functions but now was relegated to the dead. Or rather their preparation for the trip into that realm. Undertaking equipment stood everywhere, embalm-

ng fluids in ten-gallon glass bottles lined a whole wall,
planking from local trees rough-hewn with bark and splinters
erupting from them like a rash were piled up along one wall.
Bandages, saws, needles, paint, everything that one might
need to make corpses look friendly and happy for their bereaved families. Giving them the opportunity to say,
"Doesn't Tom look nice," or, "How peaceful Fred went
out," when in fact Tom and Fred and Jervis and the whole
bunch of them had gone out screaming and howling, had had
to have their guts and noses and tongues sewn back on, or
their blue skin painted with rouge and blush to make them
look like they had just been out chopping wood in the yard
when in fact they were already starting to rot, to stink up the
place. Like most service industries, a business of illusions.

Stone did a double take as he reached the center of the
place, and in the semidarkness saw a whole row of skeletons sitting up on the back wall.

"Jesus Christ," his mouth grunted involuntarily. There
was something about seeing what all of one's flesh was hung
on—just sheer, fading bone with a thousand cracks, already
turning to dust—that made you feel that you were in fact
just a passenger in this body. And two dozen skeletons sort
of magnified that feeling.

"Oh, them," Undertaker said, seeing Stone staring at the
several dozen ex-members of *Homo sapiens*. "They're dead-
beats."

"I'll say they're dead," Stone replied, managing a half
grin, which hurt his puffy lips. In fact, everything he did
hurt some part of him.

"Didn't have no money on 'em—no one would pay for
them. Now, I'm a generous man," Undertaker said, folding
his arms in front of him as he stood in front of a long metal
worktable. The bloodstains and dents of a thousand cuttings
and choppings were evident, even in the dim light of the
place. "But I run a business, not a welfare center. Man
wants to die—that's his business. But if I bury him, that's
my business. You gotta pay something—even if it's just a

damn chicken or a ring from your little finger—but you
gotta pay something or else—"

"What do you do with these?" Stone asked, pointing to
the rows of ex-citizens, which he noticed as he looked closer
were not actually all skeletons—some were only half rotted
away, the skin on their frames turned to something leathery
and dark like licorice. The lips shrunken back to threads, the
eyes squeezed down into little perfect marbles of carbon,
green molds growing over them.

"Tell you the truth, don't really know what the hell to do
with 'em." Undertaker laughed, scratching his bald head
with one of this thick fingers. "Just 'cause I can't bury 'em
don't mean I'm going to throw 'em out with the trash now,"
Undertaker explained in the same sort of lecturing tone that
he immediately took on whenever he began quoting one of
his many "truths of life and undertaking" to his children, and
whoever else he could get to listen to him. "So I just started
putting them up on the wall a few years ago, thinking I'd
figure out something sooner or later, but I ain't figured it
out." He laughed.

"Once in a while someone comes along and wants to buy
one—I don't know what for, I don't ask. Actually they're
kinda nice, ain't they?" he said, putting one hand under his
chin and studying the collection of the dead and rotting dead
on his barn wall. "Sorta like a museum or something."

"Or something," Stone muttered under his breath, and
covered it quickly with a cough. "Uh, fascinating, it really
is. I've never—" Stone was just beginning to wonder
whether the sight and presence of these denizens of the dead
wouldn't have a deleterious effect on Hanson's children
when two of them ran along the far side of the wide barn,
raising up the sawdust on the floor, playing tag among the
lower bodies chained up to the wall. One hid behind a rotting corpse and then swung it back and forth in front of him,
trying to keep his brother back. Then they both ran off
laughing and screaming as the leathery thing bounced back
hard against the wall, setting the rest of the bodies going so

that they all rocked back and forth, banging against one another like a huge, slapping wind chime of cadavers.

"Well, come here lad. Stone, it was—right, Stone?" Hanson said, slamming his big hand down on the discolored steel surface of the long table once used for autopsies in a morgue and now put to equally morbid use.

"Stone—yes, sir," Stone said softly as he started over toward the rotund man. Stone wanted nothing more than to go back to bed and sleep for about a century. But as the fat crazy man in front of him *had* in fact just saved his damn life, and since he already *had* been sleeping for about a week, Stone figured it was a good idea to just keep going— just do anything. And try not to lose what little solid food he'd eaten that morning.

"Now, I'm going to give you an opportunity here, Stone, because I like you. I'll teach you a little about the undertaking business. Something you can carry with you the rest of your life. You know what I mean—a second trade. Who knows where the vicissitudes of life will take you." From the number of dead Stone had been seeing—and creating—on his travels, Undertaker might not have such a bad idea there, Stone thought to himself. There was certainly plenty of product.

"Saw away," Stone said with a thin grin as he walked stiff-legged over to the man who was shorter than him by a good half a foot, and wider by about two. A sumo wrestler with the head of a bald Midwestern farmer with tobacco-stained teeth and the fanatical eyes of a used-car salesman. Just a typical acquaintance of Martin Stone's, Stone thought, and shook his head slightly from side to side. Undertaker took a deep breath, as if about to deliver an hour-long lecture with one intake of air, and started.

"Now, the first thing you need to do is conserve, Mr. Stone, conserve," Undertaker said sternly, waving his finger in the air like a sword about to cut off any overspender's appendages. "That means selecting exactly the amount of material that will do the job—no more, no less. That's the only way a man can make a profit. By the square inch, Stone, by the square inch."

"Gotcha," Stone said firmly, actually starting to feel just a little better as he stood there beside the fellow. Maybe it really was a good idea not to crawl back to bed, to get some blood circulating through his racked body. He tried to jump up and down slightly on his toes to increase the circulation, but after three quick jumps he felt dizzy and stopped. Exercise postponed until further notice.

"Now," Undertaker said, rolling up his thick sleeves, "in this case—and this is a slightly unusual case, I'll admit," Undertaker said with a gusty laugh. "But still . . ." He pulled the head up by the blood-soaked hair from the woven basket the farmer had left and slammed it down hard on the table like a pineapple just brought back from market. The thing bounced a few times on its forehead and then settled over on a tilt so that its eyes were sort of looking right into Stone's. Stone shifted his glance in disgust.

"But still, we can estimate what was attached until it actually arrives." He pushed the head around until it was up near one end of the twelve-foot-long metal dissecting table and set it in the middle. Then he took a long metal ruler and laid it alongside the thing, walking down the table a few feet. "Let's see, legs will be here, hips here, feet. Figure this guy can't have been more than a couple of inches taller than his *compadre* who brought him. So we'll say here—the toes are about here." He laid a second strip of metal down, this one perpendicular to the table. "Now we just take this . . ." He lifted a piece of rough wood about two feet wide by six feet long and slammed it down, lifting the head so that it rested up at the top end, facing up at the roof of the old barn, the light from the dim afternoon swirling down in halos of gold through the holes here and there in the cone above, and through the window frames, now glassless, that sat around the second and third stories of the forty-foot-high faded red barn.

For the next two hours Stone learned everything about making coffins with the least amount of wood and nails possible. About formaldehyde for pickling, about makeup for the dead, about every damn thing you always wanted to know but were afraid to ask about embalming and funereal procedures. Still, in a bizarre way Stone found it all fascinating, though his stomach kept gurgling like a sink with something stuck in its pipes.

Before they knew it, there was a knock on the door, and more of the short brown farmers were there with burros loaded down with the dead.

"Ah, see, Stone, time flies when you're having fun," Undertaker said, wiping his hands free of sawdust and chemicals and heading to the door. He helped the farmers unload their already strong-smelling baggage, and then Undertaker shooed them all out again, telling them to wait out in front by the funeral chapel—where services were conducted. The moment the door was closed again, he screamed out for his children to get the Heavenly Chapel all set up and ready, 'cause there was a bunch of ripe ones coming through.

"Now you'll see a master at work," Undertaker said haughtily. "Just keep your eyes on me if you can." He laughed, leaned over, picked up the headless body from one of the huge straw baskets, and spread it out on the table. Then he took the severed head belonging to the thing and held it until it was right in place above the stump of a neck.

"Now come on, Stone, help me, man, help me," Undertaker bellowed. "Don't stand there like a goddamn tree. Get me that hammer there, and one of them long nails." He gestured with a toss of his head to the side where shelves of tools and revolting-looking devices were stacked not very tidily. Stone reached over and got what the man had asked for and stood up again, feeling a little dizzy from the sudden rise. "Now hold this here," Undertaker said impatiently, nodding at the head he was holding firmly by the bloody scruff of the neck.

"Oh, I don't think I—" Stone smiled grimly, starting to back away.

"Get over here, mister, and help me with this. I got too much to do tonight to start playing pattycake with amateurs.

Now come on." Stone gulped and reached down, half turning his eyes away from the thing. It felt cold and wet. Out of the corner of his eye he couldn't help but see Undertaker take a long nail and place it right at the nostrils of the head. Then, with a few quick strokes, he nailed the missing appendage down right against the neck, the big tenpenny nail protruding from one nostril like a sinus dripping liquid steel.

"Okay, let go now," Undertaker commanded, and Stone released his hold. "See there?" The fat man grinned proudly. "Won't budge an inch." To prove his point, he put his fingers around the skull and twisted it back and forth. But the nail did hold the head quite firmly in place. "Now watch this, Stone. Watch close, man. If things had been different, I would have been a surgeon, I tell you. A brain surgeon, most likely, and one of the greatest in the world. Perhaps of all time." That being said, Undertaker reached down into another box of bloodstained supplies and extracted a long, nasty-looking needle. He looped a piece of nylon filament about as thick as fishing line through the eye of the needle and then leaned down over the corpse.

"You know, it's amazing how one skill can translate into another," Undertaker said as he dug the long needle into the throat of the dead thing beneath him and pushed hard. "My grandfather was a tailor—showed me a few things about cutting and sewing, I'll tell you. And really, there ain't no difference between tweed and flesh when you get right down to it." He quickly and expertly ran the needle in and out between the ring of flesh that was left hanging from the head—and the jagged stump of the neck. After sewing a circle of stitches around the connection, he stood back and surveyed his creation with pride.

"Now, is that beautiful or what?" Undertaker laughed, slapping himself with both hands against his stomach in a gesture of great satisfaction. "Looks as good as the day he was born." Which wasn't the case at all, for Stone could clearly see the terrible gash between head and body, the nylon clearly visible with its jagged, bloody stitching. But it was on there all right, it wasn't going anywhere, that was for damn sure.

The service in the Heavenly Chapel was a sight to behold. Stone sat in one of the front rows and watched the spectacle of Undertaker conducting the benedictions for the dead in a sort of cross between Billy Graham and a used-car salesman. He raised his fist to the sky, cursed the fates, told God to open his arms for some "decent folks who are comin' up", and all in all created quite a scene. His children, seated around the oak-slab benches, cried and carried on like it was their own pa who'd been done in, dabbing at their eyes with hankies and consoling one another.

When it was all said and done, the two dozen or so widows and relatives who dared make the dangerous journey from their wretched farms to the Hanson Farm and Undertaking Palace seemed satisfied. Their dead one *did* look so good—why hardly at all like he'd just had his head sawed off. And with all the pomp and noise, as cheap and as tacky as it was, they were happy. After all, all that a man can hope to get when he's gone is a moment of drama. To signify that, yes, he was worth something in this fucked-up life.

Chapter Seven _____

The dead were prayed for, anointed with precious oils, inundated with incense, which was lit all over the damn place and stank to high heaven, and last but not least, laid down in the Cemetery of the Heavenly Acres, whose motto, "Here, The Dead Don't Rise," was painted on a gigantic wooden sign that stood over the entrance to the four-acre plot that Undertaker had cleared with his own hands of every branch, rock, and corpse-eating groundhog. If not flat, the cemetery, which was fenced in all around with low stone walls, at least had the look of a real graveyard, with rows of tombstones made of larger rocks rolled into place above each grave and epitaphs sprayed on them in Day-Glo paint from aerosal cans that Undertaker had chanced to find a whole crate of.

"A suffering man lies here"

"I died 'cause my woman lied."

"Avenge me, Martha."

"I left this world a cleaner place than I found it."

"I killed Tommy Shefrin, his brother killed me."

These and numerous other footnotes of the dead were written in a graffitilike scrawl over every three- to five-foot-

44

high piece of rectangular-shaped rocks over the plots. Again, the families of the dead seemed content with the ceremony and thanked Undertaker ceaselessly as he led them off, out of the Cemetery of the Heavenly Acres. They promised to send another three dozen chickens over the next three months, a price Hanson figured was just about right. Besides, it was good for the trade to put on a show. Word of mouth spread, even when it came to dying. *Especially* when it came to dying.

Stone was unsteady on his feet after the day's events and found himself starting to fall face forward into one of the graves he had just helped dig. But hands reached out and caught him, and the next thing he knew, he was walking back toward the main house with LuAnn supporting him around her shoulder. She was looking into his eyes as he opened them, and he almost blushed from the intensity of the stare.

"Sorry, I must have blacked out for a moment," Stone said, trying to walk on his own for a moment. But finding that he had hardly any strength in his legs, he allowed her to help. He hated feeling so helpless. But all things taken into account, he was lucky he still had legs to stand on, considering how easily those heads had been detached from their owners. Flesh was so soft. Only those who killed, who sliced or cut human flesh knew its softness. It was like veal, tender spring calf—a single cut dug deep.

"Oh, Pa can work you hard, let me tell you." LuAnn laughed, and again Stone felt a surge of energy stream through him, and a heat in his stomach at the way her lips moved, the way they were covered with a sheet of moisture. "Half of us fall asleep when we hit our beds and don't wake up till the morning wake-up gong. Undertaker don't like dawdlers. He says you got plenty of time to be lazy when you're dead, but when you're alive, move your ass."

"He's got a point there," Stone replied, raising one side of his mouth in something approximating a smile. "Man knows his damn business, I'll tell you that," Stone said, liking the feel of her warm body right alongside him. Then they were at the house, the crickets chirping hard in the darkness, the moths flying into the screen door trying to reach the light of the burning oil lamps inside, occasionally finding the rips in the screens and succeeding in their fiery suicides. LuAnn led Stone up the creaking wood steps to the attic and into the bedroom, where she sat him down on the bed and he fell backward immediately, like a log ready for the paper mill.

"I'll get these off," she said, pulling off his dirt-caked boots from the digging. Then his pants. Then, before he could muster the energy to protest, everything. "Just let me wash off the old coating of herbal ointment and put on a new one," she said firmly as she went across the room and came back with a sponge and a bucket of water. Stone started to protest, not even sure why, and then just shut his mouth and enjoyed it. It felt good when she pulled the warm sponge across him, up and down his chest and stomach, and then lower. But not quite as good when she slopped handfuls of the white ointment onto him and spread it around like fingerpaint over every square inch of him. Then she toweled the whole sticky mess off and finally pulled the blankets up over his now once again white-coated physique.

"Thanks," Stone said softly. "Thanks for all you—"

"Oh, hush up," she said, putting her hand over his mouth. "You say thanks more than any man I ever met. Just what any good neighbor would do for another."

"Yeah, right," Stone said bitterly, knowing that was not quite the way it was. She rose and walked to the center of the room where an oil lamp was burning out a smoky light. She turned it down until it was just a tab of flame, emitting a tiny golden halo that throbbed out onto the walls.

Then before Stone knew it, just as he began slipping into dreams, seeing shapes in the weaving shadows created by the flickering oil flame, she was alongside him. And she was naked too. He could feel her hot flesh like a live wire suddenly touching him all along one side.

"LuAnn," said Stone in the near darkness.

"It's okay," her voice answered back like silk. "It's part of the cure." With that she reached down and began stroking him along the leg, then the stomach. Within seconds she began moving faster, and Stone could hear little groans of pleasure coming from her mouth, her lips pushed hard against his neck.

"Your work's not over," she said with a trace of laughter.

"But, LuAnn, your father, he'll—" The idea of Undertaker's four-hundred-plus pounds coming after him was not something Stone wished to contemplate.

"Oh, we all do what we want around here, are you kidding? Why, as you saw, he don't remember half our names. As long we do our share of the work, that keeps Pa happy. But I need something else to keep me happy."

"What's that?" Stone said, half desiring, half fearing the answer.

"You," she said lustily. "Ain't seen no man like you around here for a long time. Most of the guys living in these here woods got something wrong with they heads. Scared, or dumb, or some damn thing or other. But you, I like you." She rose above him and looked down at him, and even in the golden darkness Stone could see her eyes, big and wide and filled with aching desire. And suddenly he didn't care how bone-tired he was, his body was going to give this beautiful young woman what she wanted, or he was personally going to kick its ass.

But Stone's hormones were already flowing, and suddenly he had plenty of energy for whatever was called for. She rubbed her hands up and down the sides of his body, squeezing him hard, and he returned the gesture. Somehow he had thought she was inexperienced—that angelic face, those crystal-blue eyes, her tresses of blond hair. There was something about her that pulled up some image in his deep unconscious of what the ideal woman should look like. LuAnn was definitely in the right direction.

But if inexperience was what he had visualized, Stone had another think coming. The girl was like a wildcat. He was just getting going, kissing her hard, pulling her tighter against him as he found his blood starting to boil and his body go from dead to raging horniness in the space of about one minute, when she completely broke loose. It was as if a chain had been broken, a ribbon cut, a rope severed, for all of a sudden she was all over him, grinding against him as if she were a cat in heat. She made little unintelligible noises from deep in her throat and lay on top of Stone, pressing her full, hot breasts against his chest.

She spread her creamy thighs far apart and began moving up and down atop him like a snake, all squirming around, making herself ready for him. Stone felt his own manhood rising up like a flag is run up the pole in the morning, and soon he was at full staff, ready to salute and go to war. He grabbed her hard around her buttocks, which were firm but pliant, as was every part of her luscious flesh. She was soft, curved in all the right places, and strong too. Stone could feel the firm flesh as he cupped her breasts and pulled her ass, trying to bring her ever closer, harder against his own muscled flesh.

Her mouth clamped down on his, and her small tongue darted in and out like it was alive. His mouth took hers, sending his own tongue in and wrapping it over hers so she gave in to him, opening her mouth, letting her body go limp. "I'm yours," she hissed in his ear like a feline beast, with a deep, guttural, lust-filled whisper. "Do what you want with me, take me, take me." He reached down and grabbed hold of the hot, moist triangle of fur between her tensed thighs. His hand gripped around it hard, like he was grabbing a small, furry beast running across the bed. Then he slipped in a finger between the swollen lips. The scent of flowers and musk and sugary tastes swept over him as she let out a long moan and seemed to sink down onto the probing finger until he was pushing hard into her, his finger up to the second knuckle.

Then it was as if the dam completely burst, and she threw her head back and started going up and down on the raised finger like a machine. And every time, trying to take it deeper, as if his whole hand might go inside her. She was moaning all the time now, and saying his name over and over again like a little mantra, a private prayer of supreme ecstasy. At that moment she was for him—only him—with not another thought in the world.

Then she could take it no longer, so intense did her female desire become. She let out a high-pitched, catlike howl and lifted herself fast from atop him so that his hand fell away, wet and perfumed with her delicious dew. She reached down with both hands and felt for him, for his maleness. Again she seemed to go half mad, gripping at it with both hands, running her fingers up and down the pole of flesh as if she had never felt anything so exquisite before. Then she pumped at him with both fists locked tight around the organ and kept at it until Stone swore he would explode.

Suddenly she stopped and rose up over him. She spread herself apart for him and, closing her eyes, sank down atop the raised wand of flesh like an oil drill probing into the very earth. With a great scream of joy she let her body go and sank down full onto the thing until she was flat against his stomach, totally impaled by the sexual tool.

If Stone thought he had made love with wild women before, they had been like Doris Day compared to the creature atop him. For she went wild. Her entire body jerked and bucked and twisted around him. Gritting her teeth hard, almost as if she were in pain, the woman ground around on Stone as if she were trying to grind his pelvis into flour. And Stone contributed his part too. As tired as he was. As much as his muscles just didn't want to move—the instinct of desire was just too powerful to resist. After all, men with mortal wounds had been known to grab and "have knowledge of" field nurses in wartime. The most powerful instinct of all. To merge, to become one with the other in paroxysms of animal joy.

It didn't take them long. Not at the breakneck speed they were going. Flesh flying, crescendoing groans, spittle coming from their mouths. Then their breathing grew faster and faster, and their bestial noises increased and joined together until they sounded like a chorus of barnyard animals having a go at it with each other behind the barn.

Their bodies exploded together—her with her mouth

thrown far open and her eyes twitching in her head like eggs in a blender. Stone, holding her firmly as she froze above him, his eyes wide open, looking at her, taking in her exquisite young body as he poured his maleness into her in an eruption of lava. The simultaneous bursts of their volcanic passion seemed to shake the very bed beneath them, transport them to another place away from what was to a land of only what should be—the beautiful, the perfect—the orgasmic transmutation.

Chapter Eight

S tone had terrible dreams for the next few nights. Even as his body healed rapidly from the medicines and the lovemaking with LuAnn each night, the images of those beheaded farmers, of the sobbing widows and orphaned children left behind in a world that was already hard enough, all hardened Stone's own heart as well. And on the fourth morning after the burial, and a full week and a half since he'd been caught in the high-rad rains, Stone sat down face-to-face with Undertaker at the kitchen table. The kitchen children were just cleaning up. The rest were out performing their farm and corpse-preparation chores. A mother and her three young children had been chewed up by a wild dog pack. The incident had occurred just over the ridge, and the Hanson clan buzzed about it all night, constantly telling their own dumb dogs, who preferred hanging out around the kitchen more than guarding anything, to keep a special lookout that night and bark goddamn loud if they heard anything.

"Why don't you say what's on your mind, Mr. Stone?" Undertaker asked him as they both finished the last bitter dregs of Undertaker's "coffee." "You have a peculiar look in your eyes, and you been talking about nothing but them dead farmers for days, or so my young Sharon—Linda—whatever the hell her name said," Undertaker laughed.

"LuAnn," Stone said, shaking his head in amazement. It was true what she had said—her father didn't even quite know exactly who she was.

"Yeah—her. Been telling me you keep asking about how many kids they left behind, and if they had any food. And now you're talkin' about heading into Cotopaxi to pay the most murdering town in the territory a little visit. So I'm just askin' again, what's on your mind?"

"You have your skills, Undertaker," Stone said softly. "And you're damn good at them. I've learned a lot from you in these few days, but—but I have my skills, too, the skills that bring you customers. The skills of the Nadi." Stone hesitated to say it, the word that the Ute Indians who had saved his life months before had given him. Nadi—he with the gift of giving death. "So I just think I should check out a crowd that likes to saw off men's heads in front of their kids. I want to see what kind of men would do it. That's all—just curiosity."

"I've heard the name Nadi," Undertaker said, his voice changed, almost fearful. He suddenly realized he had misjudged Stone, which seemed to unsettle him. And for the first time he shut up, turned pale, and sat back just a little.

"Nadi. They don't give *that* name out too easily," Undertaker said, staring at Stone as if something were floating behind his head. "Well, then, I guess you know what you're doing. And I sure won't be the man to question it. But all the same, watch your step in there. Some of the baddest dudes around inhabit that town. And they're all looking for a fight, all looking to make a rep as the toughest of the tough. It don't take much to get 'em started in Cotopaxi. How the hell you think we get so much business?"

"That's the way I like them," Stone said with a dark grin. "Mean and dumb."

"Well, if you ever want to join on here, you got a job as

an Apprentice Undertaker. I been watching you the last few days you been helping out around here. You got good eyes, good coordination. All the right qualities to be a full-service funeral director."

"Well, that's mighty kind," Stone said, taking the last sip of the fake coffee, the only kind he was likely to see for a while. "And maybe someday I'll take you up on that if the offer still stands. Right now I got other things to do first. Like I said, making corpses, for better or worse, seems to have been my vocation for the last few months since I left my father's bunker and came topside. Not tucking them in with the daisies."

LuAnn came to his attic room as he was packing his few belongings after having just made the bed.

"Going to run off like the others," LuAnn said. "And, not even say a word. I thought you were different."

"I wouldn't have left without coming to say good-bye," Stone said, walking over to her and grabbing her around the lower part of her back with both hands. He pulled her close and locked her in a long, tight kiss. When they broke for air, she stepped away and was laughing.

"Well, I guess I *did* make an impression on you, after all," she said as she saw his eyes start to light up like they had whenever they had made love over the last few nights.

"Damn right," Stone replied as he flipped his pack up over his shoulder and started toward the stairs. "And you better believe I'm coming back here, whether I'm alive or in need of one of those boxes you all make so well, I'll be back."

"Don't say that," she said, suddenly going pale. "Please Martin. I—I—"

"Love is hard to hold right now, baby," Stone said, pausing at the door for a moment as he looked over at her, his eyes suddenly soft and vulnerable. "I have too many unfinished tasks—not the least of which is finding my sister, April. It's not a world that nourishes love, baby. I wish it were different. I wish—" He turned and started quickly down the stairs, not wanting her to see the tears forming in his own eyes.

He found Excaliber outside. He hadn't paid much attention to the dog over the last few days, other than noting that it seemed to be alive and eating its share of chow. But when Stone's attention was actually on the animal as he headed across the main yard, he noticed that it was playing with a bunch of farm dogs, shepherds, collies, mutts. Stone started ahead fast, with an expression of growing horror on his face. He had seen what Excaliber could do, and it didn't like dogs.

But as usual, just when he thought he was starting to get an understanding of the pitbull, it went and did something that totally destroyed his preconceptions. It licked the face of a huge Labrador retriever, then barked happily jumping in the air. Stone called to the animal, shaking his head from side to side as he headed toward the motorcycle. But he had only just begun to scold himself for misjudging the pitbull so terribly when it did something to completely sabotage *that* idea as well. As a shepherd got a little too close and opened its jaws a little too wide, Excaliber went down on both knees in a flash, like a wrestler preparing for a throw. He sank both teeth around the animal's lower front leg and pulled hard so the dog came crashing down on its face. They were "playing" around on grass and loose dirt, so the shepherd wasn't hurt, but the animal, which must have outweighed Excaliber by a good forty pounds, nonetheless rose and backed off like it didn't want anything to do with the pitbull. The others, too, shrank back in nervousness as the bullterrier looked around, happily wagging his tail again, confused as to what was wrong.

It was almost sad in a way, Stone thought as he whistled hard again. Excaliber turned and came rushing toward him. The pitbull was too strong, too good a fighter for its own good. And when threatened, it responded with primitive reflexes. Too bad if some little poodle got crushed into pâté.

"Come here, boy, good boy." Stone laughed as the animal began jumping and bucking around in the air as it was wont to do when in fits of extreme pleasure. "How you doing, dog?" Stone slapped the animal on the side of the head each time it reached its pinnacle of trajectory—about six feet off the ground—and it let its big tongue lap out around his wrist and arm, sending out a mini-spray.

The pitbull didn't look half bad, considering. There were still tufts of hair missing here and there, like little semibald patches. But LuAnn insisted that it would all grow back again that one of their dogs had had similar radiation burns when it explored an atomic-bomb crater about twelve miles off. The ointment she had used on it had totally healed the mutt. Stone glanced down at his own arm. It didn't look great, but most of the swelling had diminished. Pinkish bumps about the size of dimes still lingered on his back and legs. His face was back to normal, other than what looked like a bad boil along one cheek and flakes of dried skin here and there from the peeling off of his outer epidermal layers. But that would just make him look a little meaner in Murder City, which was fine with Stone.

LuAnn had told him that the boys who had saved him had found a number of burned creatures just a few miles past where Stone had been picked up. But as the kids got closer to him they said the animal life was less severely damaged. Apparently the high-rad rains had been stronger to the east and more diluted to the west. Where you were when the glowing rains hit determined whether you lived or died. Stone and the dog had been on the right side of the tracks.

"Come on, pal," Stone said as he threw his pack onto the back of the Harley, which was parked against the side of one of the barns. The pitbull jumped and came down a little lopsided on top of the seat, nearly falling off. Scampering wildly with all four legs, it managed to stay atop, though some of its hair did fly off and up into the air as it exerted so much energy.

"Damn," Stone said as he mounted up in front of the dog when the animal was at last all settled down and the hairs had stopped floating around. "Hope you don't go completely bald." Stone was thinking about how hair loss could be one

of the side effects of radiation poisoning. "Because you'll
look pretty fucking strange all pink, and with the other dogs
laughing at your pink ass wherever you go, you'll be fighting every damn second of every day." The pitbull let out a
long whine, as if it weren't at all in the mood to hear any
apocalyptic dog stories. And in a sudden mood of mercy
Stone shut up and let the throttle go on the black Harley,
which rocketed forward, screaming out a roar of power like
something that should be caged.

Chapter
Nine

The sun hovered overhead like a white-hot light bulb about to blow. Stone had to squint to see a damn thing. With the rains past, the skies had cleared considerably, but a thick haze seemed to hang far overhead, as if the gods had put their dirty linen out to dry. He eased the Harley down the dirt road slowly at first, not used to the weight of the vehicle beneath him. Everything seemed new. Stone knew he had been a hair's breadth from the other side. And now that he was back among the living, there was a sensation in the pit of his stomach like he had just been on a far-off vacation somewhere.

As Stone and his canine partner approached Cotopaxi they began seeing signs of "civilization," if that was the word for it. Dwellings were hardly more than twisted hovels with raw branches with leaves still attached to them placed over them as roofing. Stone saw collapsing buildings with ripped laundry hanging out their windows, sad-eyed women staring down from the shadowy innards. Everything was in tatters —the people he began passing along the road had their garments literally falling from their bodies. But worst of all were the faces of all whom he passed. They were the faces

of the already dead, the hopeless. Dark gray visages that
were waiting for but one thing—to die, to be taken off the
face of this miserable earth. It could be no worse in the next
life than it was in this one.

As Stone drove on a few more miles, Excaliber began
growling and snapping his tongue out at the air in lizard-
like fashion, as if he were trying to catch an insect that
had strayed too close. He soon saw what the pitbull was
anticipating, for when they turned around a bend, the road
ahead was lined with stands selling steaming pots of food
and junk of every kind imaginable. Both sides of the road
were lined with little pathetic stalls, hardly more than
pieces of wood with junk balanced around them, or an
occasional table made of hammered tin with items ar-
ranged atop it.

But it was a mockery of a real marketplace, for everything
that was being sold was of the lowest quality and functioning
order. Knives with broken blades, half pairs of shoes, shirts
with no arms, radios and TVs with all their parts and wiring
removed, just the frames left. What in God's name anyone
would do with any of it was beyond Stone's ken as he
slowed the bike to a crawl to avoid hitting any of the people
walking around.

The food, too—if it could be called that—was nothing
to write home about, either. Brown oranges, their skins
almost rotted away, individual pieces of bread with mold
growing on them, bottles of soda with only a thick sludge
left on the bottom like mud. It was a bazaar for the super-
poor, the lowest of the low. A place where they might go
and buy junk and feel like humans again, for a moment or
two, until the black horror of the worthlessness of what
they now owned hit them as they lay shivering and hungry
in their sleep.

"Here, mister, got a nice glove for you," a voice yelled
out.

"Mister, here, got socks all sizes, some even with heels
left," screamed another.

"Cat jerky here," an old woman cawed out. "Fresh and dehaired. Cat jerky—from the tail, not the paw." A rack of leather cords were strung up between two poles, and on them were hanging cats of all sizes, strips of cats like leather, paws, ears, about a dozen tails all fricasseed and smothered in some kind of sauce. Stone felt his stomach getting a little uppity, though Excaliber seemed to take quite an interest in the culinary display, his eyes opening wider than they had all morning.

"Mister, mister, you want sell dog, make good stew. Good stew—me split profits with you," one particularly ugly fellow with no nose or ears kept shouting as they cruised by slowly. Stone could hear Excaliber growling softly behind him as he caught the man square in the eyes. The appeals for the quick bucks of Pitbull Platter suddenly stopped dead, and the fellow returned to stirring his huge vat of turnip soup, which he was trying desperately to hawk to the crowds. It was not exactly a breakfast dish—or any other, for that matter. But it was all he had, so he tried to sell it as if it were precious gold. "Soup, soup, delicious turnip soup. Good for gonorrhea, cancer, and tumors of the spine."

It went on for blocks like that. And then it suddenly stopped. Stone passed a final stand, and then there were no more. The town itself stood ahead, a fairly well-developed place with two- and three-story buildings, most wood-framed, stretching off on all sides. These weren't in great shape, either, though most of them did have roofs. But as he headed the bike in and came up to the first paved street he had driven on for a while, an all black dog, quite large, with burning red eyes, sudenly darted out from an alley and sprinted straight in front of the bike, forcing Stone to pull hard on the bars and slam the brakes on. The Doberman/shepherd hybrid gave a quick glance up at the canine sitting behind Stone and gripped its load a little harder between its daggerlike teeth. Stone blanched, for the midnight-black dog was carrying a hand, a human hand, in its jaws, the wrist cut about two inches up from the base of the hand. The whole damn thing was still trailing tendrils, dripping a pinkish liquid in little splotches on the cracked concrete beneath it.

The animal darted ahead suddenly, sprinting like a cheetah, and was gone into the far alley to dine in peace. Stone stared after it for a few seconds. If God was sending him signs these days, Stone thought darkly, then he would have to say that that had not exactly been an invitation to Paradise.

He let his heart calm down as the vision of the thing kept burning in his skull like a bad dream. Then he started the bike up, seeing Excaliber staring intently down the dark alley like he wanted to go introduce himself. But Stone snapped his hand around, steering with the other for a second, and whapped the pitbull on the nose, just so he didn't start getting any ideas. With all he'd been through lately, Martin Stone wasn't in the mood to get in the middle of any dogfights.

Once inside the town, Stone could see that the citizenry had the same dreadful look as those on the outskirts had. They looked terrified, like they were afraid to let their breath completely out, their eyes darting back and forth like rats', as if awaiting attack at any moment. Drunken forms lurched around here and there as he drove on another block or two. And then they were everywhere. Men lying on their backs, their faces; propped up against the sides of the wood buildings; pissing against walls; vomiting out their guts; or just lying dead—facedown in the dirt of some alley, as if waiting to be buried only by the inevitable forces of decay.

Yeah, he was in the right place, all right. There was no mistaking it. The party was here. Seeing a bunch of motorcycles parked outside one of the many drinking establishments along the street, Stone headed over, parking his Harley in an alley just around the side.

"You stay—you hear me, dog?" he said as he dismounted. He pushed the dog's shoulders down. "Stay. I'll be back soon. If anyone touches the Harley, you have my permission to make instant human jerky. Anything else?" He looked at the animal, which stared back up through a single disgruntled eye, its head tucked between its paws and an unmistakable expression that said, "Better bring me something, asshole, something tasty or there will be tires with teeth marks in them when you get back."

Stone checked both his weapons—the mini Uzi with its long clip snapped in on his shoulder holster, and the Redhawk, .44 Mag Ruger on his hip. Between the two of them they should be able to send out some apt hellos should the need arise. Stone headed out around the alley and onto the main stretch of bars and flophouses. This seemed to be the central portion of the town as the joints were positively jumping with sounds, yells, even singing coming out of numerous, doorless doorframes and windowless windows.

Stone headed toward the place with the bikes out front. GET DRUNK HERE, a sign proclaimed above its splintered doorway, which apparently was the bar's name, as well as its function. And from the openmouthed comatose bodies all around the street in front of the joint, it seemed to be successful in its services. Stone kicked a skinny, vomit-soaked lush out of the way, who pumped both fists into the air without even opening his eyes, mumbled a few fuck-you's just to let the world know he was still there, and fell flat over on his side where he began snoring loudly as Stone stepped over his outstretched feet.

Inside, the place was a madhouse of sound and faces and stench. Stone felt like gagging the moment he walked in. A good hundred men milled around, a lot of them as foul-looking as anything he'd ever seen, even up in the deep mountains. Stone swore that not one of them had ever seen a bar of soap. It was one thing not to wash for a few days, or even a week or two if you were traveling, but these fellows hadn't bathed in years.

Stone heard gunshots and jerked, his hand starting to reach for his own tools. But as nothing ripped into his flesh, he slowed the quick draw down and raised his glance to where something was moving. A body was tied up with a rope around its neck, spinning around and around as men from around the square-shaped bar were firing up at it.

Laughter erupted here and there as pieces of the thing—its nose, a few fingers, an arm or leg—fell off. Bets were placed about what would fall next, drinks sloshed down, and the pistols roared. Apparently this was the main entertainment of the place, Stone noted as he made his way over to one of two long bars that faced each other on opposite sides of the room.

Everyone seemed huge, like Neanderthals in town for some fresh clubs. They all had barrel chests and wore animal-skin coats stitched up like the scars on Frankenstein's back. Their faces were snot-encrusted, and the foul food they ate precipitated numerous belches and farts that stank to such high heaven that Stone doubted another bear would get near them if they were tossed back out in the woods. They were all so busy bullshitting with one another that they didn't even notice Stone, a relative pipsqueak, slide through their ranks.

"Barkeep," Stone shouted, trying to catch the big, beefy bartender's eye behind the counter. After a few unsuccessful tries, the man came over and gave him a skeptical once-over.

"Are you sure you're in the right place?" the man asked. And from his twisted snout that had been broken a hundred times, and the general scarred appearance of his face, Stone knew that the man had a certain clientele in mind for his bar.

"Yeah," Stone replied cheerfully. "This is the Get Drunk, right? Well, I want to get drunk." He slammed a silver dollar down on the counter and pulled his hand away to reveal the shining coin, one of twenty he had brought from his father's stash back in the bunker. There were more there, but Stone wasn't worrying about running out of spending cash. Somehow he doubted he was going to live long enough to have to declare bankruptcy.

The barkeep picked the coin up and bit it hard. Then he sniffed it with his huge, almost piglike nostrils, which looked as if they'd been rotted way away by acid. Satisfied, he dropped the coin in a steel pail on the floor and lifted a quart bottle of something.

"Just a glassful, thanks," Stone said.

"We sell by the quart here, mister," the keep said sharply, looking at him like he had a bug on his eyeball. "What are you, a goddamn pansy? You said you wanted to get drunk? Here!" He shoved the big bottle filled with a brownish substance that swirled around in the flickering flames of the numerous lamps that had been nailed up all over the place. Stone glanced quickly around at the other drinkers and saw that in fact everyone was holding one of the big quart bottles. Some held two, taking alternate guzzles from first one then the other. There seemed to be two basic drinks here, the brown one and the green one. Stone took a sip of his brown bottle and had to do all he could not to spit it out all over the bear-size, skunk-clad thug in front of him.

After a few seconds the brew actually seemed to send out a warm glow as it flowed down his throat. Whatever else they put in the bottle, there was alcohol in the damn thing too. He turned around and surveyed the place. The bar was built of wood and was in pretty good shape, considering. There were bullet holes everywhere, and as Stone watched, the corpse target hanging from the ceiling was lowered down. It had turned into hardly more than a skeleton with a few strips of pink stuff hanging off it. The men had to have their fun. Another was strung up. This corpse looked at least three days old—the arms stiff and pointing straight out at the sides like Christ on the cross. The face and body were green, and the dead man had had a hell of a stomach, which poked out like a watermelon from his otherwise skinny and chicken-boned physique. But whatever was left of him started disappearing fast as guns were pulled, and the thing was riddled with slugs before it had even reached the rafters.

As Stone grew used to the place and started really observing things, he saw that the bar was completely segregated. On one side of the room, the far side, were bikers and their hangers-on. The men were clearly identified by their black motorcycle jackets and the knives they wore all over their bodies. On the side where Stone was, were mountain-men types, raw, crude, with the animal skin coats he'd first noticed, and immense side arms or rifles that looked like they could take out a full-grown moose with a single shot. There was an invisible line down the center of the bar beyond which men attached to either group would not step. They would step right up to it, but not over. From time to time men would come to its very edge and sneer at one another, but that was it. It was all some kind of insane game that Stone didn't quite get the point of.

"What the hell's going on here?" he asked the barkeep, who was leaning with his elbow onto the heavily scuffed counter that ran the entire length of the sixty-foot-long establishment. "I mean, these guys going to fight each other or what?"

"You're a stranger, that's for sure," the barkeep said, looking Stone up and down with contempt. "It ain't good not to know what's going on around here, pal. It's the way to get killed." Then he remembered the silver dollar in Stone's pocket, and thinking that perhaps there might be more, he suddenly softened and smiled at Stone in a brotherly way.

"But then I was a stranger once myself, wasn't I now?" Stone took a small sip of the brown mud in his bottle. God, it tasted foul. If these sons of bitches were drinking two bottles at a time of this brew, they were more brain-damaged that he had imagined. "See," the barkeep went on, leaning even farther forward and talking in a whisper like he didn't want anyone around them to notice, not that anyone would, since the target corpse in the center of the room had just taken a .50-cal. slug right in its mouth, and teeth were spraying out over the crowd, which tried to catch them for good luck.

"These is the two gangs what runs Cotopaxi. This side of the room is the Strathers bunch, the other side's the Head Stompers and their gofers. These boys hate each other, let me tell you. I mean, this town is one pie—and there's two sets of hands in it. But they can't afford to go to all-out war 'cause they both knows that they'd wipe the other one out. It's like a—you know—a stalemate or something. At least for now, until one of them can get the upper hand. They's always trying to get the upper hand. But somehow and I can't really remembers why—maybe it was when I started having the corpses up there and it became the talk of the town—anyway, both bunches of them started hanging out here. They eye each other real mean, but they don't usually go for it. Except once in a while. I guess they likes to have a neutral meeting ground to strut their stuff and make threats and sometimes deals.

"In fact, the top man of the Stompers, Bronson himself, is here. He's over at that round table far on the right there, the guy with the tattoos all over his face. And Vorstel, too, Vorstel Strathers—see, he's at the end of the bar this side. He's the one wearing the mink coat, looks about seven feet tall. In fact, he's heading on seven and a half from what I been told. Looks like his face got chew up by a bear, which it did when he was a young 'un. Give you a little advice, friend," the barkeep said with a dark gleam in his one good eye. The other was just a piece of polished marble, Stone could see as the barkeep leaned even closer and whispered conspiratorially, "Don't even get *near* them guys. I mean, don't let them hear you breathing. 'Cause I seen 'em turn on a man like a mongoose on a scorpion. Bastards will just take people out for even getting too close." He winked and pulled back as another voice called for some "green shit" down at the far end of the bar.

Stone turned and took in both of them, looking through the moving heads of the crowd so he could only see them from time to time as people shifted out of the direct line of vision. But that was enough. Both of them were bad. He could feel it in his bones. Perhaps it was part of the gift, or the curse, that told him that both gang leaders—not to mention every other son of a bitch in the place—were death-dealing bastards who he'd better not turn his back on for a second unless he wanted to find a blade sticking out of his spine.

But if the bar was the Rick's Joint for the scum of the earth, it was also a place where those looking to be "bad," wanting to make a fast name for themselves, came as well.

The killers, the gunslingers and murderers, the fast drawers
and assassins for hire gathered there. It was a tough world.
A lot of guys thought they were the baddest of all. A lot of
men were wrong.

"Hey, yo," a voice suddenly yelled out from the center of
the room. The howls and laughter of the crowd quieted
slightly to see what the commotion was as a tall, thin dude
all decked out in black leather from boot to chin sneered in
the direction of the bikers, the main table where Bronson
and some of his top boys were "entertaining," stripping and
fondling a few whores who had just been delivered to one of
their flesh houses. They stopped their drinking and squeezing of young flesh, and looked up, wondering if there might
be some amusement tonight, after all.

"I'm talking to you, tattoo face," the man shouted again,
and he tilted a wide-brimmed leather hat back and rested
both hands on his twin Colt .38s that rested in heavily em-
broidered gun belts on each side. The guy looked sharp—
Stone had to give him that. Too sharp, like something out of
an old Western, except for the leather. And though the guns-
linger would have scared half the people in the Western
world with his sunken Boris Karloff cheeks and the general
pallor of death that hung over him, Stone had a feeling that
the killer had just made the mistake of his life.

"Should I kill him, boss?" A muscle-bound, bald mon-
strosity with pins piercing his ears and nose, and no shirt
over his chest, which looked big enough to build a doghouse
in, asked his boss.

"Yeah, would you mind, Pins?" Bronson said. "I got a
stomachache—don't feel like gettin' up."

"Sure, boss," the bicep-bulging biker said cheerfully,
chains wrapped around the top of each huge bicep. "So you
want to die, scumbag?" the second-in-command Head
Stomper said, stepping from around the table. "Well, I'll be
glad to—"

If the leather-clad gunman had been waiting for the biker
to finish the sentence, it was the last mistake he ever made.
For with a blur of hand speed that was amazing for someone

his size, Pins grabbed one of the chains from his shoulder and whipped it hard out into the air. Attached to the end of the eight-foot link chain was a curved scythe about eighteen inches long. Built to cut grass, it had since had its occupation changed, but it still cut real good. The gunman, here to make a rep and a few quick bucks, had his hands on his pistols, both of them just clearing leather when the scythe, whistling like an artillery shell, sliced right into his neck. The biker had released the blade at a sideways angle, and it tore into the gunman's throat like a carving knife going into the Sunday roast. The man's whole neck just sort of exploded before he even had time to scream. His hands, still resting on the pistols they hadn't had a chance to draw, started jerking wildly, unable to lift them another inch. Then, sort of hopping sideways like a rabbit with muscular problems, the man's head tilting to one side where it had been cut by the sharp blade, the corpse-thing managed to dance around the floor for about twelve feet in a half circle before it collapsed in a bloody heap, the black leather dyed red.

The place erupted in a bedlam of cheers and screaming. The blood lust was strong here. Most everybody in the place was a murderer. And they always enjoy seeing other killers' handiwork. Pins ripped back hard on the chain, and the scythe leapt back through the air and into his hand like it was alive. He held the bone handle and wiped the blade free of blood on his brown leather, bullet-hole-ridden pants, the only garment he wore. The biker held the blade up and bowed to his boss, Bronson, who seemed bored by the whole display.

As Stone watched the bloody drama an idea suddenly took root in his head, a way to do these bastards in—all of them. It appeared in his brain fully blown, like a creature that incubates inside its egg until its an adult and then pops out completely grown with fur, teeth, and all. Martin Stone didn't know if it was the stupidest thing he had ever thought of, but he suddenly wondered if he should sign his life insurance over to the dog. Because it just might need a new mas-

ter in about one minute. Taking a final minuscule swig of th
slime in his bottle, he put it down, spat it out like mouth
wash, and stepped forward through the crowd until Pins
still basking in the glory of the killing, stood about eigh
yards away, right in front of him.

"Hey, asshole," Stone yelled out, his tongue still stingin
from the sip. Pins stopped spinning his scythe around in th
air and took a look at whatever idiot was foolish enough t
want to catch *his* attention. Stone smirked as he saw that th
man's eyes were fully on him. "Hey, asshole, I hear you
mother likes to fuck plaguers and rad mutants. I got a truck
load of them outside. So why don't you go unchain her an
we can all have some fun."

Chapter
Ten _____

"I must have got something in my ear from that leather idiot's exploding face," the biker said, slapping himself hard on the side of the head. "'Cause I just thought I heard a dumb little asshole say something so horrible to me that I'd kill me own father—bless his syphilitic soul—were he to say the same to me." The bar broke up with those words, even some of the Strathers boys let their faces move around in some sort of expression of humor.

"Well, whatever diseases your father has don't concern me," Stone said, letting his hands stay low but not obviously near his weapons. "It's what your mother got that I'm worried about." There was more laughter, this time entirely from the Strathers side of the room as the bikers faces all got ice-cold and not amused at all.

"Since I already killed once tonight, I was thinkin' 'bout lettin' you slide," Pins said as the rest of his crew and Bronson, his tattooed face staring at Stone like he was a bug that should be squashed under a boot, all watched. "But you shouldn't be sayin' those things about my mom 'cause though I look like something out of one of your nightmares,

I actually got a soft spot for my ol' mom, bless the dead bitch. And you just made me real—"

The huge biker stopped the sentence in mid-stride, and his hand whipped out the link chain with the glistening scythe on the end. But Stone had seen the maneuver once already, and he was damned if he was going to be the second butchering job of the evening. He'd been keeping his eyes dead on the biker's eyes. The Major had always told him to do that. It was just one of many tricks that Major Clayton R. Stone, ex-Special Forces, ex-Special every goddamn thing knew: "Don't look for the hand or the foot to move, always the eyes. That's where even the most accomplished of killers will reveal himself. There's always a flash in the eye just before a man strikes. Learn to see that spark of murderous intent and you can anticipate any son of a bitch out there, I don't care who he is, and take him out first." It had worked for Stone's father—the man had fought a lot of men—but he had died of a heart attack, clutching at his chest, face turning blue inside the self-contained bunker that he had had built into the side of a mountain.

Stone had always made a point of paying heed to the Major's words, even if the two of them hadn't gotten along famously. Thus he was already out of the way at the instant he saw the "death gleam" in Pins's eyes. The huge ringed hand snapped the chain out hard, and the scythe shot straight for the spot in which Stone had just been, searching for fresh flesh to mow. But it found only air swirling with the tobacco and marijuana smoke of the patrons of the filthy place.

Stone moved sharply at a forty-five-degree angle to the right, pulling up his Ruger as he slid. It was the Iaido way of walking, an opposite angle with every step, another one of the Major's tricks, things they didn't teach you at military school —or anywhere else, for that matter. The biker, seeing that the scythe had missed Stone's skull, snapped it with a flick of his wrist, and the curved metal blade, as sharp as a scalpel, whipped back two yards to the left as if it were a living predator searching for its prey.

But by then it was already too late. The hunter was about

to become the hunted. Stone ripped the huge fourteen-inch-plus chrome-plated Ruger from his holster and pulled the trigger again and again. He just wanted to stop the big sucker, who was already yanking the chain with a quick pull of his hand, trying to send the head scalper and neck slicer back the other way. The first .44 slug hit Pins in the hip and spun him halfway around like he was pirouetting in a ballet school. The second shot, a little higher, caught him mid-back, right at the spinal cord, ripping it into two twisted pieces as the steel shell tore through the flesh and bone. Pins continued to spin around like a top, propelled by the sheer kinetic force of the second Ruger shot. The third found him just about chest-high, just as he swung forward again. The screaming .44 tore right through the biker's breastbone like a drill bit searching for oil. Only what it found was red, bright red. For the heart exploded as the bullet slammed dead center through it so that Pins's brawny, bare chest suddenly looked like he had been taking a shower in ketchup.

Somehow the huge body came to a stop, and the biker looked down at the blood spurting rapidly out of the three wounds like fountains on metal cherubs peeing in a rich man's front yard, when there had been such things.

"I'm dead," he said simply and eloquently. And then he fell to the floor, his legs suddenly giving out from under him like a jack kicked away from under a stalled car. He lay there spasming, his arms and legs jerking around like manic snakes.

There hadn't been too many occasions when there had been complete silence in the Get Drunk, but tonight was one of them. Both sides of the room, both gangs, eyed each other furiously, all of them debating whether to go for their guns or not. Then they did, and every single soul in the entire place had some sort of piece or pieces in their hands, ready to send some son of a bitch into the next world. The bikers were sure that Stone was with the Strathers gang, or why was he standing over with them? The Strathers bunch, for their part, were sure that the bikers had decided to take them out and were just using this as an excuse. At any rate, the two groups of mortal enemies pulled their weapons, aimed them, and held them straight out in trembling hands, fingers pulled so tight against triggers that a fly landing on one would have set off.

But they didn't pull them. With guns aimed in every goddamn direction in the room, with just about every man clearly going to shoot someone and get shot if they fired themselves. It was like the political situation of the town itself—a stalemate. They couldn't pull a single trigger because it was pretty likely that a hundred would go off.

"You killed Pins," Bronson, the leader of the bikers, finally said with a deep sadness in his voice, breaking the stark silence of the room, which was punctuated only by breathing and an occasional burp or fart from the soused gang members of each camp. "He was like a fucking brudder to me. With me from the start. And you, you little worm who don't deserve to lick his fucking feet, you come and take him out, after all he's been through." Bronson laughed a dark, throaty laugh and rose from the table where he'd been sitting with his cohorts. The rest of them rose, too, all of them equally frightening-looking, though each in his own particular way—from chains around their necks to scars across their chests and arms and backs. Every man had tattooed or disfigured himself in some way. And they were powerful-looking. Stone had hardly seen such muscles on anybody since he'd watched his Wrestlemania tapes on VCR back at the bunker.

Bronson put both hands up on his tattooed cheeks, and Stone could see by the oil light above him that the man's whole face was emblazoned with black designs of snakes eating rats, dragons ripping girls' legs apart and biting them in a soft place. The man was sick—to the core. He was also huge, as Stone could clearly see, when the biker leader rubbed his eyes with his plate-sized hands. Not a gun had lowered; every hand still held a bead on someone across the room.

After a few seconds the biker topman took his hands away and opened his eyes. He snapped his fingers, and two of his bare-chested minions rushed down and picked up the fallen Pins, who had pretty much stopped spasming by now, his hands already hardening into a rigor mortis of clawed prayer.

"If we was alone, I'd kill you right now, scum," the biker said, burning with rage as his eyes shot into Stone's like laser beams. "But looks like if I go after you, everyone in the damn place gets turned to chop suey." He swept his hand over the bar as if it were his canvas—and the material wasn't quite stretched enough for his painting in blood, for carrying out his strokes of death. "So I'm going to take my leave, gentlemen—and assholes." He bowed a deep, exaggerated gesture, nearly stretching his head down to the buckled wood floor of the place. Stone could see by the man's flexibility and the way his muscles bulged all over the goddamn place that the biker was tough as fucking barbed wire. It didn't even look like a slug could penetrate those granitelike scarred arms. But Stone had made his move, and for better or worse, there was no turning back now.

With Bronson leading the way, guns following them as they exited every step of the way, the biker crew left en masse, not wanting to risk all their property, whorehouses, gin mills, on the turn of a gun barrel, not because of one little bastard who wasn't a piece of spit on the face of the fucking earth. Bronson paused at the door as his men filed past, holding the dead Pins aloft like some sort of sacred statue.

"You"—he pointed at Stone from across the smoked-misted barroom—"are a dead man. And on that you can make book." He spat down at the floor to punctuate the words, then turned and was gone. Outside, the sounds of motorcycles being started filled the late afternoon, and the scent of petrol fumes wafted in through the cracks in the walls. Then, with high-pitched screams and loud roars, the whole crew took off in a cloud of dust down the street.

Stone stood there in the middle of what was left of the bar crowd and felt every eye in the place on him. He could suddenly understand why actors got stage fright, as for the life of him, Martin Stone, now that he had center stage, couldn't think of a goddamn thing to say. At last, as no one else spoke up to break the silence and every gun still sort of hung out there as if wanting to shoot something, and he'd do just fine, Stone spoke up.

"Uh, howdy, folks," he said, shrugging his shoulders a little. "Sorry if I dirtied up the place."

"Who the fucking hell are you?" a voice boomed out from behind him, and Stone turned to see the one the barkeep had called Vorstel holding a sawed-off shotgun aimed straight at Stone's chest.

"They call me Preacher Boy, on account of I preach the Gospel with this," Stone said, patting his Ruger with the other hand. "And I'm here to tell you that many a man has seen the truth from the blinding light of this motherfucker."

"I say kill the asshole," said a man just to Vorstel's right, dressed in what looked like three or four bearskins sewn together the wrong way. He started to raise his chromed .45, but the leader of the Strathers gang slammed his shotgun down hard on the man's wrist, and the pistol clanked to the ground.

"You're being an idiot, as usual," Vorstel said, looking annoyed at his underling, who reached down with a pained expression for his weapon. "If it was up to you, you'd shoot every damn asshole who walked in this place. And then there'd be only me and you, and I'd have to shoot you 'cause I couldn't stand talking to no one but your ugly face for the rest of my days." For some reason the rest of the Strathers crew thought this statement was quite amusing, and laughter broke out around the place as the men slowly reholstered their weapons. Whatever was about to happen, a gunfight didn't look like it was going to be next on the agenda. But they all kept their eyes glued on Stone, who walked a few feet down the bar toward Vorstel, keeping his own hands clearly away from his weapons so no one felt threatened or got overexcited.

He could see as he grew closer that Vorstel Strathers, one of three brothers who ran the hundred-man gang, as Undertaker had told him, was truly ugly. He had seen ugly men before, ugly because their features were twisted or because of some great deformity or injury. But Vorstel seemed to have all of the above and more. It looked like he had had acid thrown all over his face and then put it through a strainer. Everything on the huge face had been moved around and rearranged, like a child's swirling finger painting. The mouth had shrunk down to something that only an olive could slide through, with but three teeth remaining in the center, so that when the gang leader spoke, he resembled nothing so much as a beaver with terrible acne atop a body that could have gotten work ripping down trees. The biggest of the Strathers brothers gave even Bronson a run for his money. Though not quite as muscular as the biker, Vorstel was, if anything, even larger and with that face, it was hard to believe anyone on the planet would challenge something that looked like that. And then Stone realized that was pretty much what he had just done.

"Why you done that?" Vorstel asked with a strange expression as he studied Stone. He walked up to him as he reholstered his own shotgun and around the stranger, giving him the up-and-down with his eyes. "Why you killed Pins? Not that I liked the bastard—in fact, I hated him—but still, what's your game, mister, Mr. Preacher Man?"

"I'll tell you exactly why I sent that man to the Lord," Stone said, getting a beatific expression on his face. He knew he had to play a part that was overdone but not ridiculous. A front that would not allow them to put a finger on him—to really see who he was. Another trick from the Major. Exaggerate an accent, a mannerism, anything about yourself. It forces the enemy to focus on that and not see the rest of you, what you're hiding, be it a plan or a weapon.

"I took out that biker bastard because I wanted to show you that I'm the baddest fucking gunner around these parts. And why you should hire me pronto, before I go sell my services to them Head Squashers, or whatever the hell they call themselves."

"Kill the bastard. Kill the fucking scumbag," voices

yelled out from around the room, and Stone heard the
squeak of dry leather as metal pistols slid out of them again.

"Put them fucking dildos away before I blast somebody's
goddamn balls off," Vorstel screamed. He whipped his shotgun straight up and let out a blast that poured right into the
ceiling, sending down a little cyclone of splinters over the
whole crew. "You guys is dumber than worms climbing onto
a fishhook." The headman snorted contemptuously. "You
won't even let the man speak before you want to kill him.'
He turned back to Stone and nodded his head, letting out a
little smile, or what Stone guessed to be a smile, as the three
teeth set in the middle of the eellike mouth seemed to curve
up slightly.

"Now, why the hell you want to work for me?" Vorstel
asked, sweeping his huge arms around the room. "I got
plenty of assholes ready to take out anyone I tells 'em to."

"That's right," Stone said, looking around the room. "Exactly—you got assholes. But what do you do when you
need someone smart, Mr. Vorstel Strathers? When you need
someone like me. Billy "Preacher Boy" Pinkus. Gunman,
negotiator, strong-arm, I do it all, Vorstel. All."

"And what the hell's your fucking qualifications, Mr.
Chairman of the Board?" Vorstel asked, looking edgy again,
like his hand might just snap up that sawed-off .12-gauge.
Stone glanced out of the corner of his eye for a place to
jump, but he knew that if his bullshit didn't work out, and
fast, he didn't have a chance in this den of wolves, every
one of whom was just itching to take his head off and send it
down to the land of unidentifiable has-beens.

"My qualifications," Stone said with a smirk, trying to act
more confident than he felt. His heart was jumping around
inside his chest like a basketball on a court, but his face
didn't betray him, it stayed hard and amused by the whole
thing. "Worked for the Chester gang out in Amarillo, the
Boffords down in Chattanooga, the Spencer twins out in
L.A., but they're all dead now, no fault of my own." Stone
spat out a ridiculous false list of his connections with other
gangs, all made up and all far enough away, he prayed, for

no one present to know the fucking difference. And no one did, for when he had stopped his spiel, the place was again silent, and Vorstel just kept staring at him.

"So you came here and killed that asshole just to get a job with me?" the face-twisted gang head asked skeptically.

"Goddamn right," Stone said. "Because I'm a man with big ambitions. "I need gold in my pocket to feel secure, and your name, the name of the Strathers brothers, is famous all over the fucking West. Everybody said you want to make big money instead of shooting the toes off every little penny-ante scumbag in the street? Go see the Strathers, they said. So here I am." He giggled softly, trying to sound like Richard Widmark in *Kiss of Death*. "I need money, big money, and you need my gun if you ever want to break the stalemate you and the Head Suckers, or whatever the fuck they're called, are in."

Stone heard grumblings all over the room but no screams of "Get the cocksucker." He stood there silently as Vorstel's eyeballs spun around in his head like roulette balls on speed.

"Famous around the country, you say," Vorstel said softly, staring at Stone. "Well, that's mighty nice, mighty fucking nice, indeed." Stone's flatteries, as he thought they would, melted the heart of even the toughest asshole in the place. All men are suckers for adulation. And he who knows it can play with them like puppets.

"Come on, Preacher Boy," Vorstel said suddenly, pushing some of his slow-moving men out of the way so that they fell backward, sprawling on the floor. "You and me is going to have a few drinks and talk about killing."

Chapter
Eleven _____

They drank for hours. Vorstel sent over for bottle after
bottle of the green and the brown stuff, and Stone had
no choice but to keep at it right alongside of the over-
grown bastard and pray that they weren't suckering him into
a trap.

"What's that on your face?" Vorstel asked him after the
first few gulps had been chugged.

"Radiation burns," Stone said, trying not to spit out the
mouthful of the foul brew he had just imbibed. If the brown,
which he had had at the bar, had been fit for pigs, the green
stuff was worse. It tasted like mouthwash in which mouths
had, in fact, been washed. Or perhaps horses' hooves.
Whatever it was, the liquid had a most unpleasant, long,
lingering aftertaste. Yet the whole damn place seemed to
swear by the "liquor," as bottle after bottle was consumed
and the barkeep kept having to send down to the basement
for more. "Got caught in some high-rad rains," Stone went
on, feeling around his face.

"You think that's something?" Vorstel laughed, pulling his
tree-sized leg up on the table, which shook around under the
weight. "Got me *this* burn when I kneeled on a piece of

metal just inside a nuke crater about fifty miles from here. I figured the radiation would be dead, but—" He pulled up the cuff of his right pant leg and rolled it up to his knee. Stone winced. The entire leg from just above the kneecap down to around mid-calf was bright purple and all scarred with cordlike knots that twisted around it in all directions. It was not the sort of leg that would win many bathing-beauty contests.

"Damn thing sizzled my skin when I touched it," the Strathers ganger went on, staring hard at Stone. "Next thing I knew, I smelt my own flesh burning, and I jumped back, but it was already done. Damn thing swelled up to the size of a garbage can. Couldn't walk on it for nearly six months. But now it works just fine."

"Well, that is a nice scar," Stone said, having taken his fifth big gulp of the green stuff, which he was discovering, to his pleasure—and horror—seemed to taste better with each sip. "But for something long and just plain nasty-looking, check this out." Stone pulled upon his fatigue jacket and lifted the black sweatshirt he wore beneath it. There was a long, narrow scar that ran from his belly button up the whole side of his chest.

"Goddamn cannibal gave me that with an ax. Can you believe it"—Stone snorted—"before I made him worm chow." Vorstel bent over and examined the reddish scar as if a doctor.

"Nice, nice, I won't say it ain't nice," the gang leader said, sitting back with a look of determination on his three-toothed face, his wisps of black hair combed over the top of his scalp like a few hurredly drawn pencil lines. "But *this* is a *real* scar." He lifted his thick black fur coat back and pulled his own thick zippered shirt back, ripping the zipper right from the material as he did so.

"Knife wound. Three guys attacked me. Then I attacked them." The blade had nearly penetrated the ganger's stomach, for there was a huge mass of tangled scar tissue that curved across the whole width of his stomach. It was almost the kind of cut one would make to commit hara-kari—the Oriental art of self-disembowelment.

"Oh, yeah, *this* was a good one, I'll tell you," Vorstel said with a wide smile. "I had to hold my own guts in while they ran and got a horse doctor who sewed the damn thing up with fishing line. But it held, didn't it?" He punched himself hard three times in the stomach where the scar tissue was thickest, then laughed loudly, screaming for more brew as he tossed a bottle back up over his head, not even giving a damn where it landed. In fact, it landed on the head of a trapper who had come down from the mountains looking for some fun. The trapper thought the bloke next to him had tossed the bottle, and so the trapper turned and cut the man's ear off with a single slice, which started quite a stir at that end of the bar, to which Stone and his drinking partner paid not the slightest heed.

"Well, you may have me beat in the 'longest' department, but I know I got the strangest," Stone bragged as some of the green drink sprayed from the corner of his lips so that it looked like he had just taken a mouthful of green paint. Stone was getting drunker by the minute and starting to lose it. But somewhere in the back of his mind he always knew where his "equalizers" were and just how long it would take him to reach them.

"Here," Stone said, lifting the back of his shirt and exposing part of his lower back. "See those five dark dots? Electrodes from an electric stun gun made them. Hurt like a motherfucker, with twenty thousand volts coming in through the goddamn skin."

"Now that's nice, that's real nice," Vorstel said with the slightly awed tone of the true connoisseur of such bodily scars. "But still I got me a weird one myself." He lifted up the pant leg on his left side and showed his own multi-pronged pierce mark, this one three quarter-sized wounds side by side in a straight line across the huge leg. "Pitchfork. Just lying there on the ground about five years ago. Didn't see it. Walked right into the damn thing, speared myself like a fucking fish. Went right through, it did. Got the same holes coming out the back too."

And so it went, as the two showed their battle scars to one another, exchanged war stories of just who they'd killed and where they'd gotten him, demonstrating it all dramatically using their hands as knives or pistols. The two "killers" got along famously, going at it until they were both so drunk that even Vorstel, who had been known to drink a cow under the table, couldn't stand up. He had some of his boys help him and Stone, and they were half carried the two blocks to one of the Strathers brothers' whorehouses, the best in Cotopaxi.

Stone kept trying to keep his eyes open to make sure they weren't taking him out back to shoot him or to just throw him down a well. In his condition he wouldn't have been able to put up much resistance. But they weren't out to get him, at least not tonight. For suddenly he was being helped into a well-lit bordello with chandeliers and purple carpets and curtains all over the place. He could hardly see what it was he was looking at beyond the bright colors, which filled his pupils like overtuned color controls on a TV set. Then Vorstel was saying good night, punching Stone in the arm so hard that it would hurt him for two days.

Stone found himself led down the second-floor hallway to one of a number of rooms that lined both sides. Two Strathers underlings threw him down onto the plush bed inside, turned out the lantern, and left, nodding their heads back and forth in disgust that this scum was being treated so good by Vorstel. But he was one of their top bosses. Not one of them would dare question an order from the man, or from someone Vorstel considered to be a "friend." They had all seen what the topman could do, and it wasn't something they liked to think about.

Chapter Twelve _____

S tone was asleep and in a drunken stupor by the time he
hit the satin sheets of the featherbed. He slept hard
through the night, sunken deep into the bed, his face
mashed into the pillow. When he awoke, it seemed like he
had only been out a second, but he had a headache the size
of the Grand Canyon. Why had he drunk all that slime water
last night? The sheer memory of it made him want to puke
his guts out. Stone pulled his face out of the pillow,
squeezed as flat as a pancake into the mattress, with the
night's drool covering its case. He turned over and tried to
look around through the half-closed orbs that felt like someone had been frying eggs in them.

He had a dim memory of purple rugs and drapes and,
opening his eyes fully, saw that it was true. For the whole
room was done up heavy-duty, as a bordello circa 1890s
New Orleans. The room was lavishly overdone with mate-
rials of velvet and satin-colored deep purples, magentas, vi-
olets, and cherry-reds covering every wall, chair, bed, and
window. A gilded mirror hung on the ceiling straight overhead, presumably for the occupants of the bed to witness
their writhings in the post-video world. Stone got a good

look at his rad-pimpled, stubbly, hung-over face, and it wasn't a pleasant sight.

Suddenly he remembered Excaliber. He had left the damn dog outside, guarding the Harley last night. The realization slammed into his already reeling skull like a sledgehammer pulverizing a piece of rock. Stone groaned and fell back down, wanting only to slide under the satin sheets and sink into sweet oblivion. Anything could have happened. The damn dog could be dead, the bike stolen. And it was all his fault for going into the Get Drunk and getting soused to the point of no return.

"Fuck." He cursed at the walls, gritting his teeth. He rose, and since he hadn't taken a thing off when he was deposited on the bed, not even his boots, he didn't have to put a thing on, either. Without even straightening his hair or flattening out a single one of the hundred rumples and creases on his clothes, he tumbled out of the bordello room like a wild man from the mountains who hadn't yet been domesticated.

Most of the early-morning staff hadn't arrived yet, as it was only 6:48, so the place was nearly empty downstairs but for two old women who polished all the woodwork in the place, keeping it shining for the "gentlemen" customers. They looked at the savage-looking Stone and shuddered, looking away, wondering silently to themselves just how bad the place had gotten if it was taking in clients of such low repute. Perhaps they'd better start looking for jobs elsewhere. The Hot Vagina might not be the kind of place they wished to work anymore.

Stone stumbled outside into the early-morning daylight. Just his luck, the sun was shining like it was about to nova, the air was brilliant, the light cutting down like a sheet of shimmering aluminum foil from every pore of the crystal sky. He had to walk along, holding his palm over his eyes, which only added to his bizarre appearance so that the few people walking the streets of Cotopaxi veered away from the madman who was praying from his eyeballs. Stone wasn't even quite sure where he had left the damn bike or the damn dog. They had dragged him blocks from the bar. But at last a few things looked familiar. Then he saw the alleyway. Taking a deep gulp and holding his breath, for Stone was truly terrified that he'd find nothing, he walked to the alley entrance and turned, his stomach clenching up like a fist.

The dog was there. It was all right. It was standing atop the Harley and staring straight ahead at the entrance of the alleyway like it was ready to kill any son of a bitch who even showed his face around the corner.

"Uh—uh—sorry, dog," Stone said, sidling forward, trying to lift his shoulders apologetically but finding that the shrug made his neck feel like a guillotine was being run through it. "Ran into some trouble, you know how it is." The pitbull didn't say a word in return. Not a growl or whine or snarl. Nothing. And that got Stone more worried than he had been. For he had never seen the animal completely silent before. It stared at him with black, brooding, accusatory eyes the closer he got, giving him looks of, How could you, you slime-sucking pea-brained moron and I'm going to kick your ass when I feel like it. And other such canine expressions of high-level indignation.

"Look, dog—okay, I fucked up. Give me a break. You fuck up, too, sometimes. Remember how you jumped off the fucking Harley and went after a whole pack of timber wolves? That was great. Now you conveniently forget about that." The pitbull stared back at Stone, not giving an inch. That was history. "Okay, okay, look, I admit I fucked up," Stone went on, seeing the merciless, unforgiving look in the animal's eyes. At last it let out a little snort of contempt through its dry and hungry muzzle, which to Stone was an encouraging sign.

"I know, I know, you didn't eat all night, and dozens of assholes tried to come in here and steal the—" As he spoke, Stone saw something on the filthy alley ground that showed that someone *had* in fact tried to come in. A finger, a human finger, freshly bitten off, lay at the foot of the bike, still oozing a little rivulet of watery blood.

He grinned at the dog, which refused to return such a look

but stared only harder, as if trying to burn its canine anger into Stone's soul. "All right, come on, Mr. Macho," Stone said at last, seeing that he was dealing with a brick wall. He took out the chain leash that he had used a few times on the animal, quickly snapping it around the pitbull's collar. The animal pulled at the thing with a whine and then bit at it with his jaws, but Stone pulled hard, full steam ahead, and the animal jumped down from the bike and quickly followed, trotting along at his heels.

Stone led the dog back down the street, appearing even more demented than before, since he now had an equally odd-looking creature following right behind him. If this was what they were breeding up in the mountains, thought dozens of townspeople who were out to open their food and used-goods stores, someone should go up there and wipe the whole damn place out.

Back at the Hot Vagina, Stone walked right up to the madam, an ancient thing with so much pancake makeup and red rouge on her face that she looked like something a child had colored in a coloring book.

"I want a steak," Stone said. "A steak for me, and a steak for my dog here. Make that two steaks for my dog, and eggs too. Right up, okay? And two glasses of stout or beer, but none of that green or brown stuff I had last night."

"Breakfast for two." The madam smiled without batting one of her four-inch-long eyelashes. "And will the two of you be needing any female companionship?" she asked, looking first at Stone and then at his dog.

"We're into steak and eggs, sugar." Stone grinned as he suddenly saw himself in the gold-edged mirror and realized what a pig he looked like. Back upstairs, he found that the plush room had a real bathroom with—amazement of amazements—a bath with running warm water. Stone had no idea how they did it, but he didn't ask. He took off his things while the pitbull sniffed around the perfumed chairs and couches of the main room, his nose going wild with the thick, overlapping smells.

Stone washed all the slime and the last coating of medicine off him, not to mention the blood he had splattered on his hands the night before when he had taken out Pins. Afterward, dried off, his hair combed back, he looked at least like he belonged to the human race, if not one of its outstanding members. The food came just as he had slipped his boots on, and Stone and the dog gobbled up the steaming chow like there was no tomorrow. The animal took half its plate down in one immense bite, turned its brown-and-white head to the right, where it drank its glass of foaming, home-bottled beer with one big slurp, spilling half of it over onto the floor. Then it swung back to the dinner plate, a china-blue pattern around the edges, and lopped up what remained in a single wet snap of its tongue.

Stone was hardly through his third forkful when the canine whined from across the floor, where its plate sat empty, and looked at Stone with an Is-this-it? kind of expression.

"Forget it, dog, you can't have a fucking single bite of mine. That's right, not one bite. I know, you wished now you'd eaten that finger instead of spitting it out last night. But that's how it is. Now, please, go meditate or something, I don't need dog drool over my eggs." The pitbull retreated, sulking to another smaller bed across the room where it jumped up onto the powder-blue satin covering and found itself a nice spot in one of the feather pillows, stomping it down here and there until it was just right for the shape of its body. It let out a deep sigh, then its head fell back and the big tongue lolled out of the right side of the furred face. It had been up all night guarding the bike, hadn't slept a single moment. And it hadn't been just one offending hand that it had had to snap at.

Stone finished his breakfast, and his stomach actually began to settle down. He vowed never again to drink anything brown or green. Then he checked his weapons, making sure they were both loaded and in full working order. He had a feeling that his nine-to-five job as a hired killer was about to begin. Sure enough, there was a knock on the door, and Stone opened it to see one of the bearded underlings of the Strathers gang.

"The brothers want to see you now. Pronto!" the man said, clicking his teeth in an obscene little sound. "Over at the Paradise Girls. You know where it is?"

"Yeah," Stone replied frostily. The man shut the door and was gone. He chained Excaliber's chain leash to the railing of the brass bed that the dog was lying in like the King of Siam. Then he headed out, trying to close the door softly so as not to awaken the animal. He didn't need any more accusing stares of desertion. On the way out, Stone stopped by the front desk and threw the madam a few silver dollars.

"That's for me and my dog for the next few days. Have another plate of steak and eggs—no beer—sent up in an hour or two. Oh, and this is very important, tell whoever brings it not to go inside but to just leave the food inside the door and then close it fast."

"Will do," the madam said with a curt smile as she turned back to the ancient, yellowing romance magazine she had read over and over a hundred times so that its pages were covered with her fingerprints from makeup and lipstick. Stone kept expecting her to at least question some of his requests. But apparently a lot stranger things went on around here than a dog having breakfast.

He made his way back to the main stretch of the town and to the headquarters of the Strathers clan. Stone could instantly see which was the place, as about a dozen of the lower echelon were set up outside a four-story building with a sandbagged machine-gun emplacement. It was all very official-looking, until Stone noticed that the guys had the ammunition belt inside the weapon upside down. He didn't have the heart to tell them. Besides, someday soon they might just be firing the thing at him.

When he gave his name at the barricade, he was quickly ushered in by a low-level slime whose low-sloped brow and hairy face and arms wouldn't have been out of place about two million years ago when *Zinjanthropus* had roamed the world.

"De brudders will see youse now," the man said, trying to sound official, which was just about the most ridiculous sight Stone had ever seen, since the filthy fellow had dried snot and bones from last night's alley-cat dinner all over his rabbit-fur vest. This particular group of rabbits looked somewhat the worse for wear what with bullet holes and bloodstains all over their pelts. Not that they were complaining.

"Thank you so kindly," Stone said politely, figuring it couldn't hurt to make a few "friends" around here.

"Ah, Mr. Preacher," a voice said from inside a room. Stone walked in and saw three men seated side by side in large, plush armchairs—the Strathers brothers. And off to one side of them, chained to a wall, was a full-grown lion— mane, claws, teeth, and all.

"Uh, hello," Stone said, feeling like a whole swamp of frogs was stuck in his throat. "Nice lion you've got there." He grinned and walked into the room, keeping a nice distance from the creature, which was eyeing him either hungrily or suspiciously.

The Strathers brother nearest the beast, a smile on his thin face, reached down and stroked the animal along its golden mane. The predator closed its eyes and let out a roaring purr that sent goose bumps up Stone's backbone. He headed quickly for the one seat they had left available, a similarly ornately carved armchair facing the three of them. Stone sat down in it, and once he saw that the lion was not about to leap at his face and rip it into sausage patties, he let his stomach loosen about a millionth of an inch. He turned toward the three brothers, who were staring at him, six sets of eyes burning through the brightly lit room with its row of windows, letting in golden streams of the morning sunlight.

"So, Mr. Preacher Boy—what's the fucking story?" the brother fondling the lion asked him. Stone made a quick take on the three to see just who the hell he was dealing with. Vorstel was on the right and he was smiling, at least it looked like he was. In the light of day his twisted, acid-burned face looked even more horrible than it had when he had drunk with the bastard the night before. The one in the middle was about a foot shorter than Vorstel—from the description Undertaker had given Stone of the three, this one was Rudolf—but the man was no less formidable, being about as wide as a table, with no neck and hardly a chin to speak of, either. Stone always tried to find his enemy's most vulnerable spot so that when and if he had to, he'd know where to go. But he couldn't find an Achilles' heel on this one. The man looked like he had armor built over him— nothing had been left exposed, nothing open. Just rock-hard muscle and belts of ammunition that crisscrossed back and forth over his broad shoulders.

The third brother, Jayson, was the smallest of the three, smaller than Stone himself, who at six-foot-one, was no slouch. But the man was thin, like a rail. Stone was sure he was a junkie, judging by the emaciated cheeks, the white lips, the thin smirk that junkies always had right after they'd just shot up. The brothers would sure as hell have access to it all. Stone saw something else, too, in the fraction of a second that he let his eyes sweep across them—that Jayson was looking back at him with something more than a killer's curiosity.

"My story is, as I'm sure Vorstel here told you," Stone began, "that I've come here to make a name and some god-damn money for myself. And I've chosen your organization to do it. I could have picked those other bastards, you know. I mean, ultimately it don't matter to me. But I heard good things about you guys. That you run a tight ship, that as long as things are kept in place, the money flows like water out a spring." The three looked flattered as Stone again used the oldest trick in the book. Men will believe the most obvious lies about themselves if they are made to look good.

They seemed to digest Stone's words for a few moments, no one in the room saying a word. Stone had no way of knowing if they believed everything he was saying, or if they were about to launch Simba, Son of Tarzan, over there, right into his kidneys.

"And just what makes you think you're the man what can keep things in order here in our sweet little town of Coto-paxi," Jayson asked him, taking out a dab of some powder in a perfumed silk handkerchief and sniffing it greedily into his inflamed nostrils. It was a bizarre mixture of men—the two huge Cro-Magnons on one side, the effete dandy dressed in a monogrammed red morning robe on the other, his legs up on the edge of his chair as if he were riding sidesaddle.

Stone smiled grimly. "I just know. That's all." He let his eyes fall on each one of them for a few moments, to let them feel his will and to let them know that he wasn't bullshitting, that he *had* killed men and could do it again.

Suddenly he saw a flutter of motion from Jayson's handkerchief and then felt a sudden rush of energy from behind him like something attacking. Stone instinctively leaned forward, crouching fast, and the assailant behind him, already striking with a baseball bat, fell forward so that he tumbled over Stone's head, and the bat cracked down on the floor in front of the chair. Stone was up in a flash, grabbing the hand with the bat and at the same time placing his right foot down on the slime's neck, locking the man so that he was completely immobilized. Stone pulled up hard on the arm, and the man let out a howl of pain. Stone raised up the bat with his free hand, ready to let the sucker's head feel what a home run felt like, when a voice yelled out.

"That's enough, Preacher, you don't have to kill him." It was Jayson, retrieving his handkerchief from the floor. "It was just a test, man. Just a test. All done in a spirit of friendly paranoia."

"Just a test, my ass." Stone snarled angrily. "My brains would have been all over the fucking carpet if Junior hadn't struck out there."

"If he'd hit you, Mr. Preacher Boy, then you wouldn't be the one we want, now would you?" Jayson asked with a mocking, effeminate tone in his voice as he tilted his head and looked coyly at Stone. Stone let the attacker up, and the gang member ran from the room, a look of confusion on his face at the speed with which Stone had moved.

The three men conferred with one another, leaning in so

that their heads were almost touching. They whispered for about thirty seconds, then sat back and faced forward again.

"All right," the neckless one said with a deep, grinding voice that sounded like he ate gravel for breakfast. "Youse is hired. But watch your fucking ass—or youse won't have one."

Chapter Thirteen _____

"**T**here's just one other thing," Jayson said with a look of quite disturbed pleasure on his made-up, concave face.

"Yeah?" Stone asked, sensing something nasty in the offing.

"The initiation ceremony into our gang." Jayson laughed a hideous little squeaking effeminate laugh that contained no humor. Then his eyes rested on Stone again, like a rat's on a baby's face. "It's really quite simple," he said. "You just donate some of your blood to our—godfather."

"What is he, from Transylvania?" Stone asked with a smirk, not feeling like giving to the blood bank today.

"No, no." Vorstel laughed, his three teeth—one above, two below—grinding together as a wet sound emerged from within.

"See, everybody needs an angel, you know something to watch over dem so's dey don't get rubbed out. You know super-superintendent-type stuff."

"Supernatural, supernatural, you asshole," Jayson screeched out, wincing. His brother's constant misuse of words seemed more than anything else to be the main source of friction between him and the two illiterates. "He means *supernatural* protection, Mr. Preacher Boy. Protection from a divine source. You should know about that. After all, you're a preacher."

"What I preach, men don't want to hear," Stone said with an icy look.

"Well, we all have our own gods," Jayson replied cheerfully, sniffing more powder up his nose from a straw hidden behind the red silk scarf that he dangled across the lower part of his face. "But if you want to join our organization, you must give to *our* god." He rose, and the lion lifted its huge head, looking around to see what was going on and if there was trouble. Seeing that absolutely nothing of interest to its sensibilities was in fact occurring, the great, golden-maned head sank back down again like a rock onto its folded paws where it fell within seconds back into a semi-dream state where it was mounting a female of its species and giving it to her real good.

"Yes, over here, Preacher Boy. Over here." Stone rose and joined Jayson, who had walked toward a separate smaller room off to the side. The two other brothers rose, as well, and followed. Their presence right behind Stone set him on edge. He kept thinking about the distance from his hands to his guns.

"Yes, we keep our shrine in here, right here in our headquarters, so we can have constant access to him." Stone followed the emaciated leader apparent of the brothers into a bizarre chamber filled with candles. It was like a religious shrine; a thousand burning candles set on numerous shelves sent out flickering golden flames, making the room appear almost as if it were on fire. It was almost like walking through the very tongues of flame. On the floor was a red carpet, thick and plush, and ahead, up on a pedestal, was a bust of a man. Stone walked into the room, as if he were walking into a bad dream, and followed Jayson over to the huge plaster head.

"This, this is our god, our inspiration, Al Capone," Jayson said, making a little bowing motion with his head as his

two brothers did the same behind him. Just to be on the safe
side, Stone tilted his head just a notch, so they could at least
interpret that he had genuflected if they wanted to. He stared
up into the plaster features of the sculpture. It was very real-
istic-looking. Whoever had made it—and from the faded
coloration of the thing, he estimated it was at least forty,
fifty years old—had done a good job. It also appeared that
they had had up-close access to the most famous criminal
who'd ever lived.

The face looked evil. There was a sneer on the sculpture's
face that bespoke someone who could snuff out a life with a
laugh, slam a baby's head to the sidewalk with a chuckle.
The bust seemed to be composed of death, as if the artist had
injected the very energy of Capone's soul into the sculpture.
The jagged scar along one cheek that ran almost an inch
deep didn't help make the guy look any friendlier. Nor did
the eyes, which, even from the depths of the plaster figure,
seemed to try to pull Stone down into them, to fill his mind
with a sudden rush of dark and grotesque thoughts and de-
sires.

"Here," Jayson said, snapping Stone from his momentary
fixation on the bust, which was standing about five feet off
the ground on a miniature plaster Roman column. "Every
man in our gang has given his blood. . . ." He pointed down
to a small bowl that was filled with what looked like about
four inches of congealed blood, turned almost black now
like tar. "It's our way of giving something to Al, so he gives
something back."

"Well, I don't know," Stone said, backing away from the
revolting little collection pot. "I'll tell you the truth, I don't
have a hell of a lot to spare, and I'd pretty much like to keep
what I've got."

"Just a little," Jayson said with a pout on his concave
face. "A few drops—surely you could spare that." The
other two brothers, towering over him like bears, stood just
behind Stone, looking nervous and concerned.

"Well, I guess I could part with a few drops," Stone said

with a dark expression. He walked forward until he was just above the gruesome altar.

"Here," Jayson said, holding out a hand-carved dagger with a beautiful marble blade. "It's sharp."

"Thanks, but I'll use my own," Stone replied, stepping back from the silk-scarved brother, who had a stench about him of old perfume and other things. He pulled out his own blade, a foot and a half of razor death, and held it against the fatty part of his forearm. His body was already so blasted to pieces, another notch sure as hell wasn't going to hurt anything. Stone rested the blade right against his skin and pulled lightly. The edge of the blade was so sharp that it dug right in, and Stone squeezed the small gash so that a few drops fell and landed atop the dark purple gum of blood in the bowl. He looked up, and Capone's mouth seemed to be twisted up just a little higher at the corners.

"And now the oath," Jayson said with a little hysterical giggle, as if he were moved to tears by the ceremony. "I swear to kill whoever the Strathers brothers tell me to. Or may Al himself come back from the grave and crush my head with a baseball bat."

"I promise to kill whoever the Strathers brothers tell me to," Stone said, stepping back from the bowl and wiping his cut on his pants as he replaced the blade. "Or may Al himself come back from the dead and crush my head with a baseball bat."

"There, that wasn't so bad, was it?" Jayson asked, reaching out as if to pat Stone on the shoulder. But he moved just out of the way of the fake-fingernailed hand. He didn't want that slime's flesh to even touch his.

"No, not at all," Stone said, moving away from the altar and circling around just a few steps so that they weren't surrounding him anymore. It was instinctive with him to always position himself, always be prepared to strike, parry —or get the fuck out of there.

"Now, just one final little thing," Jayson said, clapping his small hands together. "The other part of the initiation." Stone looked bored for a second, wondering if he was going to have to drink more of that green or brown, or maybe slurp down a little blood. Yeah, that would hit the spot.

"You have to kill someone." Stone's face paled, and he coughed and took a few steps so that they didn't notice. "All new applicants to the gang must kill a man to become full members. Besides, you've killed dozens, right?" Jayson said with a mocking look that instantly made Stone suspicious of the guy.

"Bring him in," Vorstel screamed out, cupping his hands and shouting toward the doorway. In seconds a struggling mountain man—one of their own gang—all chained up hand and foot so he could only move a few inches at a time, was escorted in. He was brought before the three brothers and his legs kicked out from under him so he slammed face-first down into the rug. Then his hair was pulled up so he was raised to a sitting position, looking straight at the statue of Al Capone.

"He stole shit from us, from his own gang. Nobody steals from us. Kill him," Jayson said, folding his arms across his chest and looking on in an expectant manner. Stone gulped hard, raising his hand to his mouth as if picking his teeth to disguise his nervousness. He couldn't do it. He couldn't kill a man in cold blood no matter what he'd done. In combat, yes—he would take out anyone who tried to take him out. But just to execute someone on orders, no way. He never could do something that cold-blooded. Stone tried to think fast. The brothers were starting to look at him. He knew they'd kill him at this point if he refused to play along any further. And he knew that in the small space with all three of them—and a fucking lion—he didn't stand a chance. His mind raced like a computer as he tried to think of a way out. What would the Old Man have done? What the hell would the Major have done if he—

Stone took out the Ruger .44, raising it slowly up into position. Suddenly he had an idea. It was risky, but he had no other chance. The brothers watched as Stone sighted up the man's head, and they got an excited look in their eyes.

They loved to see men die. Next to raping virgins, it was their prime pleasure in life.

Stone got the man's head in line. The pathetic bastard was crying, tears flowing out of his puffed-up, wart-edged eyes. He was an ugly, murderous slime. But still, the pitiful bastard deserved to live. Stone wasn't going to play God.

He shifted the gun fractionally and squinted. This was going to have to be the best fucking shot he'd ever made in his life.

"This one's for you, Al," Stone said, and pulled the trigger as the slug tore out of the muzzle with a roar. The bullet ripped right along the side of the man's skull, sending him flying sideways from the sheer force of the hit. Though it didn't actually penetrate the skull, the bullet did rip a nasty wound along the skin and the thin layer of muscle up there. A curtain of red poured out around the head as the man slumped to the ground, motionless, knocked out into deep freeze.

"You got him good," Vorstel mumbled inanely. And Stone saw as he glanced around quickly that they were all excited by the killing. These bastards made the Marquis de Sade look like a nun.

"Yeah, I always get them good," Stone said, slamming the Redhawk back into its leather home.

"Feed him to Pussy," Jayson half shrieked in excitement as he clapped his hands and two men came forward to drag the still body away, a small pool of blood extending out around its head.

"Uh, wait a minute," Stone said, walking forward so he was between the body and the rest of them. "Look, let me have the corpse. After I kill ʾem, I like to cut ʾem up in private, you know?" He looked around at them. He was taking a wild chance that the bastards were so sick that they *did* know what he was talking about. And he was right. Jayson looked hard at Stone, for he in fact had his own private ceremonies with corpses that only he and the devil were privy to. That Stone was on the same wave length as him almost made Jayson like Stone, at least for a second or two.

"Sure, take him," Jayson said. "Have fun with him. There's lots there to cut up." He laughed. Stone leaned over and grabbed hold of the 250-plus pounds of ganger and threw him over his shoulder in a fireman's carry. He walked forward, staggering slightly under the weight, with the three brothers following behind. Jayson closed the door to the altar of death behind him, to the thousand candles burning brightly like the marbled eyes of corpses in the moonlight.

Stone walked out of the place with the "dead" man, praying that he didn't come out of his unconscious state in front of the brothers, or both he and Stone would quickly learn all about the real thing. But the thug stayed dormant, his head coated red from hair to chin like he had been dipped in paint. Stone walked about three blocks, making sure none of them were following him, which, as far as he could see, they weren't. Even those slimy bastards believed in letting a man carry out his perversions in private. He saw a stable with a few horses tied up in front of it, and a familiar-looking cart with a few coffins on the back. It was one of Undertaker's, with the big *U* on the side in gold paint, which marked all his funeral equipment.

"Hey, boy," Stone said, hissing up to the kid who sat in the high wood-plank seat reading a dirty magazine he had just rented for a penny from a dwarf who sold them from a "newsstand," a shack with two sides and no roof across the street. "Psst, boy, wake up," Stone said, staggering now under the weight of the man he'd been supposed to kill. It would have been a lot easier to take the son of a bitch out, that was for damn sure.

The kid looked up like he was pissed off to be torn away from his dirty mag. "Huh," he said with a buck-toothed mouth, looking at Stone with a somewhat idiotic expression.

"You one of Undertaker's brood?" Stone asked.

"Sure am, mister," the kid began. Then he remembered Stone from the farm, and his face took on a slightly more intelligent look. He threw the magazine down under the raised wooden seat of the wagon. "Hey, what the hell you got there?"

"Now listen to me," Stone said, "and listen carefully." He lowered the man off his shoulder, and the unconscious body fell forward with a loud thud onto the flat wooden back of the wagon next to two coffins sitting there. "This is very important. Take this sucker out to your spread. Tell your father the bastard's not dead. He's one of the Strathers gang. I was supposed to bump him off, but I didn't. Tell Undertaker to fix up his head and then kick him the hell out of there. The guy knows he'll die if he comes back, so he won't. You got all that, boy? You understand what I'm telling you? And don't let him move until you're out of town. No one except your father can know he's still alive."

"Sure, I understand," the lad said, glancing around at the limp body behind him.

"And this is for your trouble," Stone said, taking out a silver dollar that everyone in the territory seemed to love more than life itself.

"Hey, thanks, mister," the teen said, flipping the coin in the air and catching it in his palm. He pulled the reins hard, and the big old mare hitched to the front started lazily and grudgingly forward, one snaillike step at a time. "And if he wakes up before I'm outa here"—the Undertaker kid grinned, revealing a whole row of missing front teeth, then hefted a large wooden mallet that looked like it could drive stakes into the ground—"just call me the sandman."

Chapter
Fourteen

That evening, now that he was on the payroll, Stone was sent out with some of the "collectors" to see how things were done around Cotopaxi. It was agreed after some hard negotiating—and Stone pushed it to the limit, wanting the brothers to think that he really was a greedy son of a bitch who was after every stinking penny he could get —that he would receive a basic monthly stipend of fifty silver dollars. And an additional thirty-five for every asshole he had to kill. Workings-over were only fifteen dollars. Mass killings, when necessary, would be charged by the half dozen at the rate of two hundred dollars a dozen. All proceeds were payable upon delivery of body, or any part thereof. Then they all shook on it. And after making sure he still had his fingers, Stone was part of the operation.

Ovan and Mr. Tibbets ran the little search-and-collect mission. The two guys reminded Stone of something he had seen in a bad dream—one of them with an ear missing, the other with a wide scar that looked like it had been carved by a steam shovel running across the front of his face, almost level with his lips, so that it looked like he had a perpetual Cheshire-cat grin. All the Strathers gang members seemed to be in dire need of some sort of physical repairs—their teeth were half falling out, there were sores all over their skin and hands. Coming down from the mountains to run the show here hadn't improved their health habits or their appearance, though the thugs Stone walked down the street with at least had cleansed their ragged clothes—fur jackets and vests—of food and bodily fluids.

The first stop was the butcher shop, which Stone could smell from half a block off, and the meat didn't smell the freshest. As they drew closer, he could see the dark carcasses on racks in front of the place. Inside were all kinds of chops, steaks, rumps, from bear to wildcat, horse to dog. A group of old ladies and housewives bickered and jockeyed in line for the precious cuts. Their faces froze up in fear as they saw the Strathers boys walk in.

"Ah, Benchley," Ovan said, walking over to the butcher, who was dicing up a big alley cat. He was slicing the fur right off the carcass and throwing it in a basket with other blood-coated pussycat hides to be cleaned and made into clothing and blankets for his wife's apparel store across the street. He moved the cleaver up and down the skinned alley cat like a Japanese chef making sushi cutting the cat into little inch-long pieces for stews and shish-kebab.

"Benchley, Benchley, how's it going?" Ovan said with a big smile. A less sincere expression was hard to imagine, as his scars somehow made his face look like a mask, a demonic exaggeration of a man actually smiling.

"It's going . . . okay," the butcher said as the whole crew of little old ladies scampered out of the place and down the street. "Not too good, really," he said softly, finishing his last slice and burying the cleaver in the wood cutting board, coated with a waxing of blood. "People's poor now, can't buy meat like they used to. . . ."

"Now, didn't look like that to me," Ovan said, looking around for the old ladies, a few of whom stared through the half-cracked window of the place and then rushed off as the gang lieutenant caught them with his ratlike eyes. "Looks like you got every ol' bitty in town buying a roast for her old man." Ovan leaned over the cutting board and picked up one of the freshly carved cat squares, popping it in his mouth and chewing it down fast.

"Mmm, good. You should really market these on a wider scale," Ovan said, taking a few more in his pocket for later snacking. "Now, where's the dough? We ain't even been around here for two weeks, got caught up in other stuff. Let's see . . ." He pulled out a little notepad on which were scrawled all kind of unintelligible figures. "That'll be one hundred dollars."

"One hundred dollars?" Benchley repeated, growing pale as beds of sweat popped out on his forehead. "That'll ruin me. That's about all I made in the last two weeks. One hundred and sixteen dollars. I swear. I mean, I don't mind paying you guys money for 'protecting' me from the Head Stompers, but all of it? It's too much, too much."

"Too much, is it?" Ovan started forward, and from behind him, Stone saw the thug reach for his spiked brass knucks, which would have caved the butcher's face in without much problem. Stone suddenly moved forward, getting in the way of the gangman, and ripped the cleaver from the meat table. He pulled it back and threw it hard, and the cutting tool spun through the air like a missile, whizzed by Benchley's right ear missing it by not more than three or four inches, and buried itself blade first about three inches deep in the wall behind the man.

"I'll get it, I'll get it," he screamed out, his face draining of every ounce of blood. It was one thing to be poor. It was another to have a meat cleaver poking through the center of your skull, opening it up for all the world to see. He reached down in a floorboard, lifted it, and pulled out a small package wrapped in brown paper. He handed it over to Ovan, who took it with that same horrible, fixed smile.

"Well now, that's mighty kind, mighty kind," the collector said, counting the coins and bills inside. "Now, you just keep cutting your meats. And by the way, I'll be sending my whore to pick up something tonight, so have something nice for me, okay?"

"Yes, Ovan, I will, absolutely," the butcher nearly sobbed. "The best." He stood there quaking in his boots as the crew walked out, grabbing pieces of meat from here and there and chewing them on the spot. No gourmets these, but then where they had come from in the mountains, men had been known to grab squirrels from trees and eat them live, ripping off the heads, chewing them down, then spitting out the clumps of fur that were left.

They headed outside and down the street. "That was pretty good," Ovan, the collector, said to Stone as he fell in alongside him. "You didn't even have to smash him."

"I believe in pure fear," Stone said, holding his fist up in the air and turning it over. "If you can throw the fucking fear of God into the other guy, he'll do whatever you want, you don't even have to slug him."

"But, I mean—" Ovan stuttered, looking a little confused. "Don't you miss it, you know, caving in people's noses and chests? I mean, it don't seem natural."

"Saves my knuckles, my hands, for the things I really need 'em for," Stone replied. "After all, my fingers are precious commodities."

"Yeah, I guess that's true," Ovan said with a metaphysical glimmering in his dark eyes. He held his own fist up and turned it in the air like a precious jewel. "'Dis is my tool of my vocation. If I broke dese, I wouldn't be a very good collection man, now would I? A handless collection man— it don't make sense." He looked at Stone with a new respect and saw why the brothers had hired the guy. He had it up top.

The next store they came to was the barbershop, where nearly two dozen local townspeople were lined up to get a shave in the one barber chair that sat in front of an old broken porch. A barber pole, one that looked like it had been around when Abe Lincoln was president, stood alongside the chair, although it no longer revolved or even lit up. But the motionless spirals of red and blue and white that twisted down its side still gave the signal to all the world: Hair was cut here.

This time it was Mr. Tibbets, the second-in-command, who went up to the barber, an old white-haired fellow who was snipping away at a man's hair.

"Hair today and gone tomorrow, hey?" Tibbets grunted out, which was the same thing he said every time he came around to the barber, thinking it was pretty smart each time. "You got my taxes?" he asked, the thin smile vanishing from his face. "You was behind last time. Let's see, that's"—he took out a notepad—"twenty-nine dollars and seventy-three cents. But seeing as how it's Barber's Week, I'll let you keep the seventy-three cents." He looked around at the crowd of cowering men, there for their yearly trim. "And don't let no one say that the Strathers brothers ain't generous men."

"Yes, I h-have it right here," the barber stuttered. "I got it, I got it," he went on in a panic, reaching into the torn white smock around his chest and legs. "But not all of it—I couldn't get it all. It was a bad week and—"

"Pal, pal," Tibbets said, slapping his hands together in front of him so they made a loud cracking sound and startled all the haircuttees, making their faces twitch in fear. "I'm not sent out to get excuses, you know what I mean? I mean, I'm just a working guy like you. I go back to my boss, I tell him *I* don't have *all* the money, it's my ass in a sling. You understand, right? So . . . the money?" He held out his hand and stared at the barber with a frozen face.

Shaking, the man handed over a small packet of coins to the collector, who went through them, then looked up, his face growing red. "I said money, asshole, not chickenfeed." He leaned over and picked up the scissors the barber had put down on a table a few feet in front of him. Remembering what Stone had done with the cleaver, Tibbets pulled the cutters back and let them fly. He had intended for the long scissors to go into the rotting wall behind the man, but they went into his stomach instead. There was a sickening wet sound, and they all looked over to see a spreading pool of red right in the center of the white smock near the barber's waistline. The scissors were only in about an inch, so the barber was clearly going to live. But either the pain or the blood got to him, because he slipped to the ground in a dead faint.

"Take care of him," Tibbets screamed to the waiting customers. "Tell him that next time the scissors are going all the way through—unless he's got twenty dollars more." He slammed the twenty dollars or so worth of change that the man had given him into his pocket, and the Strathers crew headed on down the street to the next poor bastard who was working his balls to the bone for nothing.

And so it went through the afternoon. They must have hit a total of forty stores, for the town serviced a large area of the territory—people coming in from all over to get supplies, haircuts, knives, spices. Stone didn't know if it was his influence or not, but at least he was able to prevent anyone from being killed or seriously injured, although a number of throats were squeezed, a few noses broken. He did what he could.

By the time they returned to headquarters and the two team leaders brought in the loot, they must have amassed over a thousand dollars, a staggering amount for a town that was so poor. These bastards were bleeding them dry. Not content to just blood-suck off them, they wanted to drain every last penny out of the place, make the people who lived and worked in the entire area slaves to them. The poor suckers were caught between a rock and a hard place—the Strathers brothers and the Head Stompers. God only knew how they paid off the bikers when they came around.

He split from the collections team and headed back to the bordello and bed. His feet were aching from the day's walking—they must have gone twenty miles up and down every street. He hobbled into the place and up to the madam, this one a younger and much thinner one, who smiled up genuinely. Evidently his showering and hair combing earlier had worked wonders.

"Where's the big mama?" Stone leered down at the woman, who sat behind a cherry countertop. She had immense breasts, which hovered out over the counter as if ready to plop down on it.

"You mean Mama Creole? She don't come on till midnight. I'm Tessie, five-to-midnight shift. What can I do for you, mister? Drugs, pussy, food . . . ?"

"Send up a steak—no, better make that three—and potatoes if you got em, anything. Room 210."

Her smile suddenly faded from her red lips. "You the guy in 210? Damn, mister, what the hell you got in there, a sea monster or something? We been hearing all kinds of noises and horrible sounds coming from up there all day. Mama Creole tol' me you had some kind of dog or something. But didn't sound like no dog what was making the noises I heard. I tell you, a man went up to see what it was, and something came flying at him, all teeth and snarling. No one would go back there again. Whatever you got in there, mister, get it out of here. Please. This is a high-class joint. We don't allow bloodletting, or sacrifices, or—"

"Calm down, calm down," Stone said, but he knew it had been tantrum time again for Rin Tin Rip. "Just get them steaks up to me," Stone said, starting toward the stairs, "and I promise you the creature won't eat none of your girls." The woman's face got even more flustered, but Stone was already gone, taking the creaking wooden steps three at a time. He paused at the door and knocked twice, then twice again, the signal he had taught the animal to recognize him by, or so he hoped. He knew the pitbull might try one of his patented jump-leap-snap-bites first and ask questions later.

Stone gingerly opened the door, ready to leap out of the way. His eyes grew wider and wider with every inch that he pulled the door back and could see inside. The place looked like a Titan missile had hit it. It was a total and complete shambles. Every bit of the beautiful drapery was ripped down and chewed to pieces, every rug and wall hanging was in tatters, covered with drool. But it wasn't just that. No, the furniture, too, had been attacked, as if by a psychotic elephant. The posts of a sofa and the legs of three chairs had been chewed to near splintered oblivion so that two of the big velvet settees were leaning over on three legs. Snapped and twisted pieces of wood and metal that were no longer even identifiable were scattered around the room. The dog had clearly had its fun.

Stone walked inside and saw the entire brass bed to which he had chained the animal, moving slowly along one wall as if the damn thing were haunted. For a split second Stone was filled with a deep fear and thought he saw his mother's dead face shimmering in the air. But then his rational mind realized instantly what it was, and the irrational vision faded away like a dark dream into the pits of his soul.

"Okay, dog, I get the idea, you're pissed off, right?" The bed dragged along another foot or so, the entire frame and mattress being pulled by the pitbull, which suddenly appeared from around a chair set on its back, legs dangling in the air like a turtle that couldn't right itself.

"Didn't like being chained up, I can't blame you. I know you're an outdoors dog. But we're doing, you know, undercover work here, dog. I can't be taking you around with me all the time, you hear? It would cause problems."

The dog rounded the corner of the chair and came slowly toward him, loping along like an old mule dragging an entire house behind it, which, considering that the bed was about ten times larger than the animal that was pulling it, was not an inaccurate proportion. It came right toward Stone, the bed catching on the chair and pulling it along, too, just part of the debris that had accumulated around its brass legs as it had been dragged around the room.

"Dog, I told you from the start, you weren't always going to like traveling with me. *You* asked to join *me*, remember? Or am I getting my facts wrong? Don't I remember a poignant mutt standing at the foot of my motorcycle in the snow just begging not to be left behind? And now, look what you do to me. Dog, you hear me?" Stone said firmly, raising his voice. "You've got to become more civilized." The animal stopped at his feet as if delivering the bed and stood there frozen, like it just wanted to stand there and would remain so for a thousand years if it felt like it.

"Oh, shit." Stone snarled, muttering curses under his breath as the dog continued to fume, staring straight at the door as if he were in a trance. It took Stone nearly half an hour to get the place straightened out enough to be habitable. He unchained the pitbull and rechained it to a cast-iron antique wood-burning stove sitting atop two immense bear-clawed steel feet that sat at one end of the room and must have weighed at least six hundred pounds. Stone sat back on the bed and just waited for the animal to try to pull that over. Instead, it lay down and stared at him like some accusing six-year-old whose cookies have just been stolen.

But before Stone could get too depressed about the whole situation, food arrived. He sat back on the bed, chewing slowly, and tried to figure out just how the hell he was going to pull off this whole insane plan. And whether his ass was still going to be attached to his legs in another day or two. Excaliber, not being the kind of creature to learn from experience no matter how often it is repeated, ate his entire platter of steak and homegrown squash in about the time it takes a lizard to down a fly with its snapping tongue. Then he lay down and eyed Stone's platter with lust in his heart.

Chapter
Fifteen

It was the Fourth of July. If Stone had forgotten about it, he sure as hell was reminded of it by a hand-cranked record player that turned out tunes from the old days: "America the Beautiful," "The Star-Spangled Banner." It was absurd. For it was "America the Ugly" now, and "The Blood-Spangled Banner." But still, Stone felt a stirring in his chest at the tunes, played slightly too slowly, and echoing up and down the street like a cackling joke.

He sat up in the bed, realizing he had been dreaming about April. She was being... He didn't want to think about it. It was as if thinking about it might make it happen. It was the ancient fear of the primitive—that his very dreams would come true. Before Stone blew him away, Alamoso, the mafia gunner, had told him she'd been taken by the mob. But they wouldn't hurt her. More likely the mob would treat her with kid gloves. For Stone knew they would use her as bait to lure him. And he would come as surely as a dumb fish rises to the lure.

But he had to do something here first. Stone was realizing, as his father had before him, that his responsibility fell to more than just his own blood. If he did have the "gift" to kill, if he was in fact the last of the Rangers, carrying on all that his father, the last man to give a damn about freedom and slavery, good and evil, had taught him, then it was beyond Stone even to dictate his own life. He was caught up in a web that was bigger than all of them, one that would decide whether America turned to complete barbarism or rose again out of the ashes, the pits of bones, the rivers of blood.

He rose up, aching, his body still not quite used to work, to movement. The walking around of the day before had made everything in him get all shook up. But though he felt stiff and still a little feverish, he was definitely heading back toward the living. It was amazing what LuAnn's goo had done for him and the dog. Stone glanced over at Excaliber, who was sleeping at the foot of the bed, the long chain draped around him leading back to the railing of the brass bed Stone slept on. His fur was already growing back in the numerous places in which he had been burned. It was a little whiter than the rest but it was filling in nicely. Still, the damn mutt was starting to get scarred up, like Stone. They were both dogs of war.

Stone got up, trying not to rouse the pitbull, as he knew it would start demanding things. He got into his clothes, strapped on his pistols, and headed to the door. It was only half open when a whine from behind stopped him in his tracks. Stone turned with a sheepish grin, since he knew that the dog knew that he had been trying to sneak out on it. The animal looked at Stone skeptically and licked its lips, suddenly getting up and challengingly starting to pull the brass bed an inch or two.

"All right, all right, for chrissake, you little blackmailer." Stone closed the door and headed down, wondering if there was a good dog-obedience school open in the neighborhood. He told the day madam downstairs, the cute one with the pixie nose and tits that would have made watermelons feel inadequate, to throw some more steaks into the room. He pulled out ten silver dollars and tossed them down onto the counter.

"That's for the curtains, chairs, you know," Stone said,

looking a little embarrassed. The damn hound was starting to cost bucks. The madam took the glistening coins and looked at them with a primal lust. Then she kissed each one and dropped it between her ample bosoms, the cleavage big enough to hold a whole bank.

"Tell me," Stone said, scratching his face and realizing that he was starting to look like the Abominable Snowman again. The madam pulled back an inch or two, as if Stone had fleas. Which, come to think of it, he suddenly realized, feeling itchy all over, was not at all impossible. "What's all that racket outside? The Happy Marching Murder Band?"

"It's the Fourth of July, mister. What you been taking?" She looked askance at him, as if he were completely and totally out of it. "Biggest celebration we got here in Cotopaxi. The one day of the year that the two gangs—the Strathers and the Head Stompers—have a truce. No fighting or killing allowed on this day. No, sir. But lots of drinking, shooting contests, all kinds of stuff. It's fun, a barrel of laughs," she said, looking forlorn. "I just pray I ain't gonna get stuck here all day, 'cause the bitch who's supposed to sub for me at noon says she just got a sudden 'big' customer and will be on her back, so to speak, for hours."

"Thanks," Stone said, heading out. "And feed that damn dog, or the walls will start going too." She clicked her lips, as if the animal were becoming the disgrace of whore row but went quickly into the kitchen where a Chinese chef began throwing horse steaks on the griddle, heavy on the soy sauce.

Stone walked outside, the glare of the day not sending quite as jarring a shock into his eyes as it had yesterday. He could see right away what she meant. It was a real celebration. Banners were up, hanging across the street from sagging window to falling frame. Vendors were already out selling their crow pies, their snake burgers, their tripe soup. . . . The entire main street, nearly twelve blocks long, had been barred to all traffic—motorcycles, mules, horses —and crowds of people who had come down from the surrounding wilds were already filling the streets. After all, it was all that was left of the old America, of days when there had been hope.

Stone walked around sampling the various wares, sniffing carefully at the pots of bubbling food, checking whether the stuff was poisoned. He figured if it didn't smell rancid and had been cooking hard for an hour or two, it couldn't kill him. So he sampled nearly half a dozen of the strange delicacies.

It was going to be a scorcher; he could see that already. Men had stripped down to their waists as the noon sun beat down like a heat lamp in a sauna. Stone took off his fatigue jacket and tied the arms around his shoulders, pulling his T-shirt out, trying to ventilate himself a little better. Then he saw them, the Strathers brothers, just at the midway point of Main Street. A long table had been set up for them, and the three brothers, along with a dozen of their top henchmen, sat there smoking cigars, drinking, and looking altogether like the well-to-do murderers, thieves, and warlords they were. The area around them, for about fifty yards in each direction, had been cleared of all the normal clods and morons from the mountains. The reserved area was just for the crime bosses. It was the VIP lounge of the bloodletting set.

Stone walked up to some of the nasty-faced guards who stood along one side, holding the crowds at bay. The ganger started to raise his shotgun as Stone walked up but turned and caught a nod from Vorstel at the table. He let Stone go by, looking at him like he would just as soon mow him down.

"Howdy, Preacher Boy," Vorstel said, rising up as Stone came over. "Please, please take a place at the table here." He pointed to the right, indicating that Stone should sit at the end where the brothers sat, which was clearly an honor. They were going for his Preacher Boy creation, Stone could see—hook, line, and sinker.

"Oh, Preacher, you really should have shaved," Jayson said, looking even more effeminate than when Stone had seen him the previous day. The thin, greased-hair brother was wearing a purple smoking jacket that hung down over his shoulders like a Liberace costume and, around his neck, an ascot with red and pink dots. He looked bizarre, not that all the other frog-faced slime were any beauties. "You know, we all *do* try to turn out our best on the Fourth. Man needs some traditions, you know." Jayson arched his neck and stared at Stone like a feline.

"Yes, yes, sorry about that," Stone said, sitting down to the right of Vorstel. "Been traveling so much, doing so much killing, haven't had the time to shave a lot of the time. Get out of the habit. You know how it is."

"Ah, let him alone," Rudolf snarled. His bulldoglike head had a wide-brimmed gangster-type hat atop it. "I didn't fucking shave, neither."

"Yes, but you've got no face, dear brother," Jayson said, batting his eyelashes, which Stone noticed were fake and quite long. "So no one can even tell." He laughed sharply, and the entire table looked at the ninety-five-pound amphetamine-and cocaine-addicted transvestite like he should have been thrown in a garbage pit.

A beat-up whore dressed in something resembling both a Roman toga and a Betsy Ross getup, only with her breasts sticking out of two holes that had been cut in her "Colonial" costume, came over to Stone and handed him two bottles, the green and brown stuff again. Stone thanked her and put the foul brew down on the table, hoping no one would notice. Suddenly there was a roar of engines to the east, and every eye turned that way as the crowd a few blocks up parted, screaming and jumping out of the way for their very lives.

The Head Stompers were coming in like the forward batallions of Attila the Hun. Three dozen motorcycles in a phalanx formation, modeled after the Roman legions. They rode atop their bikes, standing on the seats, steering the things with strips of leather, which they wrapped around the handlebars on each side and then around their hands. They could drive the things like trick-riding cowboys in a rodeo. As they got to within a few blocks, Bronson, who was at the lead point of the phalanx, whipped the chain

from his shoulder and spun it around his head like a pro-
peller blade. With the long scythe on the end, the whistling weapon created a shimmering circle of silver in the
air. The biker leader looked like an apparition, an envoy
from hell, towering above the seat, his bald, tattooed head
gleaming, his huge, muscled body like something carved
out of titanium.

Stone could see the Strathers clan all around him start to
go for their weapons as the bikers approached to within a
block, letting go with piercing war screams as they surged
forward in a stampede of thundering machines, with oily,
black smoke rising up behind them. But at the last second
Bronson stopped his bike on a dime, whipped the chain back
in so the links wrapped back up around his shoulder, and
jumped off the motorcycle, all in the space of about two
seconds. Stone gulped hard. The man *was* tough. The rest of
the biker crew came to a halt in even rows behind him, all in
near perfect formation. Then they, too, jumped down,
snapped down their kickstands, and headed over to the table
across the street from the Strathers, where they sat and
glared over.

"Happy Fourth of July to you, Mr. Muscles," Jayson
screamed out in a piercing falsetto.

"And fuck you, too, scum," Bronson screamed back,
slamming his fist down on the table, and a whole squad of
whores came running with brew and drugs. Stone was impressed with the level of conversation around here—this
was a bunch that could really make you think.

But the men didn't waste words, they went at it—partying,
that is. And after an hour or so, as the drunken orgies began, as
the whore-fucking contests went on, with women tied down on
long tables with men pumping away at them, as all manner of
perverted and deranged Fourth of July contests were carried
out, Stone could see that these guys really knew how to
celebrate. And when both sides of the street had drunk enough
to sink a battleship, the main contests began.

The shooting contests were the one chance the two com-
peting gangs got all year to have a go at one another without

slitting each other's throats. It was a way of relieving tensions, getting things out, a competition to see who was best —for *that* year, anyway. Any man from either gang was eligible to compete—if he had the balls. After all the elimination rounds there would be one winner, who would receive a trophy with a pistol on top of it. It was an old beat-up thing, gold-plated at best, with the .38-caliber casting of a pistol atop it cracked in five places. Yet every man there coveted the broken NRA trophy and would have given anything for it, for in this little fucked-up portion of the world, anyway, it was the symbol of the highest achievement and respect.

At one side the crowd was pushed back by the guards, and Stone saw three platforms being wheeled in. They were huge affairs, like miniature gallows on wheels, and hanging from each of them, with a rope around its neck as if it had been hung, was the stiff corpse of a cow. It took ten men to push each of the cow contraptions, but at last they had them in place side by side, about fifty yards from the opposite sets of tables where the gang members sat.

Stone watched in fascination as the first round of firing began. Three at a time, men from each gang would walk up to a line that was drawn on the street, and when the judges said, "Go!" they opened fire on the things.

"Head!" one of the judges screamed. And the three contestants fired madly at the head of their respective dead cows; .38s and .45s and .9-mms blasted away at the huge, furred corpses, sending them spinning and jerking around wildly. Eye sockets disappeared in a storm of blood and bone; ears were drilled off; noses turned into oozing swamps of red.

"Chest," a judge screamed through a megaphone. The gunmen lowered their aim, the chest cavities erupted in gushes of pink and brown. The center of the beasts were opened up, the rib cages splintering out like broken umbrellas, the hearts cut into party appetizers that exploded out the openings as if looking for guests to serve.

"Legs," a judge commanded after about ten seconds. The

fire shifted lower, making the thighs of the things jump
around as if they were trying to perform some arcane rock-
and-roll dance. Within seconds one of the competitors had
completely severed the leg of his cow, and it dropped to the
ground. Stone could see the judges making little notations
on notepads as they figured out the scores for each man.

And so it went for nearly two hours, as gang member after
gang member tried his luck. Stone, too, entered the fray,
figuring what the hell. He easily worked his way up to the
top ranks and then was one of the final three contestants.

The three men were called to the line: Stone; One-armed
Carter, the best marksman of the Strathers; and Bronson,
who had won the coverted award the year before, and in
fact, had it tied to the front of his motorcycle. The three let
their hands dangle loosely at their sides as fresh cow bodies
were brought in. When they had totally stopped swinging,
one of the judges screamed out, "Head!" And the butcher
shop of slugs was on.

Stone had opted for the .44 Mag. The Uzi was really for
taking out bunches of men, not cows. But Stone knew that
the .44, when placed just right, could do the trick. While the
other two opened up fast, as if trying to impress the judges
with the rapidity of their fire, Stone slowly took out his
Redhawk, raised it in a smooth arc, and sighted up the cow,
dead center between its eyes. It was the Major's method:
Better to take aim and hit something in two seconds than to
get five shots off in one and miss every damn one. By the
time the others had already squeezed their trigger five or six
times, Stone pulled lightly on the hair action of the .44. The
skull of Stone's cow snapped back like a cannon shell had
hit it as the slug entered the big head just two inches down
from the eyes and dead center.

It was as if the stress point of the entire skull had been
shattered, for the whole center of the big brown-and-white
hided face just sort of disappeared, and stuff bubbled out all
over the place. Not even wasting a second shot on the thing,
as there wasn't a hell of a lot left to hit, Stone looked to see

what the judges were doing. But they just scribbled away without looking his way.

"Chest," the judge screamed out. Stone sighted up carefully with the red-dot floating sight system down the long chromed barrel of the Ruger. He pulled the trigger, then moved the .44 to the right and down and fired again, then fired a third shot, making a triangular shot pattern. The slugs tore through the air, whistling like teakettles about to explode. They slammed into the chest bones about a foot apart and seemed to rip the whole center section of the cow right out of it. It was as if a saw blade had just been drawn in a jagged circle about a yard wide as the bones erupted out, opening the floodgates for everything wet within to come gushing out onto the street, creating an instant sea, yards wide, of cow intestine and organs. Again Stone stopped firing. He slammed a quickload into the Ruger and had it all loaded up again before the judges yelled, "Legs."

This time Stone was extra careful, sighting up right at the juncture of thigh and body, while the other two were blazing away madly, like the gunfight at the OK Corral. Stone pulled once, and the lower right leg fell from the huge, swinging carcass. He swung the Ruger to the other side and fired twice in six-inch spacing. The left one erupted in a rain of gristle and bone fragments, hung for a second or two by a few big arteries, and then dropped down to the street below, where it splattered hard against the ground.

Stone raised the .44 up to the upper legs of the huge, blood-spattered beast and fired twice more. Both of them flew down to the broken concrete street as well, like tap dancers looking for work. Stone slid the monstrous pistol back in his hip holster and stood back waiting as the two gangers continued to blast away like they were reenacting the St. Valentine's Day Massacre.

It didn't take long after the firing had ceased for the judges to make their decision. Stone's cow was a limbless parody of a creature, without legs, without a chest, without even a face anymore. It just hung there, a huge piece of red protoplasm, turning slowly in the hot breeze. It was just what the judges were looking for, after all. Total and complete annihilation through firepower. No, there was no choice at all—the trophy went to Martin "Preacher Boy" Stone.

Chapter Sixteen

Just about everyone was pissed off at Stone—Bronson, One-armed Carter, all the gang members from both clans. Who was this scumbag to come out of nowhere and claim what was rightfully theirs? The only people who seemed genuinely pleased by the whole turn of events were the three Strathers brothers themselves, who saw that Preacher Boy's winning, and the fact that he worked for them, was already starting to swing the balance toward the Strathers. Not having his men blast Stone to death on the spot back at the Get Drunk was one of the best things Vorstel Strathers had ever done, or so he kept mumbling to himself all afternoon as he got drunker and drunker.

But the cow target practice was only the half of it. According to the Strathers brothers, the big fun would be that night. They wouldn't tell Stone exactly what the fun would be, they just encouraged him to come, bring some betting money, and watch the sport of a lifetime. Stone hung out until he couldn't hide the fact that he wasn't drinking any of the green or brown, so he split, not wanting them to think he wasn't carrying out his hard-drinking Preacher Boy charade.

He walked around sampling some of the evening's culinary wares. Though all the cooking pots of the peasants who had come to sell their particular recipes were stained and bent, many of their dishes were actually quite tasty. Stone got stuck on fried rattlesnake tail dipped in batter, deep-fried, then rolled in white sugar. It was like nothing he'd ever had before. He wasn't even sure if he liked them or hated them, but he quaffed three down before he moved on.

His intestines started to do their own snaking around as the afternoon's food intake hit him like a ton of bricks. He walked with a strange expression on his face through the crowds, seeing an occasional fistfight here and there, but no killings or severed arteries. Such was the law. Any gang member that broke it was subject to death. Just the year before, Bronson had shot one of his men on the spot right on Main Street for slitting the throat of a lower-echelon Strathers man who had spit on his boot.

Back at the whorehouse, the night madam gave him an extremely bizarre look the moment he opened the door.

"You," she said, staring at him like he had just turned Jesus in to the Romans.

"Me?" Stone said, looking back at her as he walked across the blue-carpeted floor with its erotic images of men and women doing extremely obscene things beneath his feet. "What did 'he' do now?" Stone asked, not wanting to hear the answer.

"You mean, what didn't that damn demon dog do," the woman replied, shaking her head from side to side like she thought she had seen it all, but she hadn't until today. "Do you mean the girl he bit on the hand who tried to give him his food? Do you mean the sounds that emanated from up-stairs all day, scaring half our customers out the door? It's hard to screw when a dog is eating all the furniture and howling continuously as he gallops around pulling a whole goddamn bed behind him. I don't know if there's anything left in that room. No one's been in there all day. Mr. Preacher Boy, isn't it?" She smirked skeptically, and Stone knew she was on to him in some way. Something in her eyes told him to be real careful around her.

"Look, here's another ten," he said, shoveling out a bunch of silver dollars that rolled around on the countertop. Again the money seemed to help, as the woman's eyes lit up like a wino who'd been handed the keys to a liquor store.

"How long you planning to stay?" the madam asked, trying to smile but not really able to.

"Not more than two or three days," Stone said, trying to look mean at her, make her think he just might shoot her if she messed with him too much. After all, he was a hard, bloodless killer.

"Let's say two days, Preacher Boy, at the most. We're letting you stay here 'cause you're a personal recommendation of Vorstel. But even that only goes so far. Two days at tops—and you've got to chain that animal and muzzle it, or shoot it, or some goddamn thing. You hear me? That psycho hound's gonna drive me outa business."

"Chain 'em up—absolutely," Stone said with a smile as he headed up the stairs on the trot. "Absolutely." He reached the second floor and threw open the door to his room—and held his breath. It actually wasn't that much worse than the previous day. But then everything had pretty much already been decimated the day before, anyway. Today the pitbull had been mostly working on truly grinding down what it had ripped apart into wet splinters and odd-shaped little pieces of chair legs, lampposts, and couch arms. Feathers from pillow stuffing were spread out over the entire room like a duck graveyard, and Stone sneezed even as he walked in. The animal had even managed to bend a few of the vertical two-inch-thick bars that formed the backboard of the huge king-size brass bed.

"All right, pal, I get the message," Stone said as the bed started heading through the debris like the fin of a shark circling its prey. "You don't like being locked up. Well, I can't blame you." He spoke softly, suddenly seeing the whole thing in a different light, from the dog's point of view. "When I found you, you were locked up inside a Plexiglas cage and you didn't like that, did you, dog? In fact, I think that's what I actually admire about you, you homicidal maniac, that you fight to be free—right through the walls if you have to." As he glanced around the room, Stone saw that indeed the pitbull had taken a few big bites right out of one of the walls, so that huge gouged holes sat there, wood lathing all cracked and bent in and plaster hanging off in clumps.

"All right, dog, get your dancing shoes on, 'cause we're going partying tonight." But this was easier said than done. Undoing the dog from the bed, Stone wrapped the leash securely around his wrist five times. If the canine took off, it would have to drag him along behind it. He headed downstairs, and Excaliber strained wildly at the leash, dying to get into the real world, real air, and out the perfumed chamber where he had been slowly going mad. The night madam shrank back in horror as the pitbull came charging down the stairs, snorting and drooling like it was a bull heading for the ring.

"Get him—get him—out of here!" She gasped, putting her hand to her throat, but Excaliber was already out the door, gasping for the outside air as he pulled Stone forward like a sled dog. Outside, the animal immediately did a series of leaping, bucking high jumps right up into the air. It was as if he had been so confined that now he had to completely release all the pent-up energy in the wild leaps. Some of the people walking by slowed down, keeping their distance, watching the mad dog as it twisted and flipped into the air like a dolphin out of water trying to flop its way all the way back to the ocean.

"Come on, pal," Stone said after a minute or so, "we're drawing a crowd." He pulled the dog hard and nearly had to half choke the damn creature to get it to pay attention and follow along. Stone saw another dog about a block ahead, walking behind a man on horseback. He pulled hard on Excaliber's leash just as the pitbull charged forward with its teeth bared and a loud snarl. The other dog, a collie, shrank back in horror and ran to the other side of the horse, figuring it would have to get him first.

"Jesus Christ," Stone spat out, pulling the animal hard so

he had it walking right alongside his hip. He spoke down in a harsh whisper to it. "Listen, mister, I said I'd take you to check things out if you behaved. We haven't gone one block, and you're attacking everything with fur in the fucking neighborhood. Now come on!" He stared hard into the animal's eyes, and it seemed to comprehend, snorting out an unhappy compliance with the rules. But it did seem to calm down after that, and trotted happily along next to Stone, its tongue hanging out in the sticky night air. Ah, sweet freedom.

Stone followed the street around to the Strathers' headquarters and then to the back. The closer he got, the louder it got. By the time he actually turned the corner of the building, he heard what sounded like the bloodthirsty crowd for a bare-knuckles boxing match. There must have been three, four hundred men all standing around a huge pit dug in the earth about twenty by twenty feet square and perhaps ten deep. Stone could see that the bikers were on the far side, and the Strathers gang on the near, all glaring at each other and throwing curses and insults back and forth like balls at a tennis game. In the flickering flames of numerous torches and lamps set up on stakes in the ground, the scene was quite primeval, and filled with the promise of blood.

Stone made his way over toward the pit, not having much trouble getting through the crowd once they saw the pointed-face cannonball of chiseled dog hide coming toward them, his muscles rippling up along his thighs and back with every step. Stone walked to the edge of the pit, looked down—and gasped. It was the lion. The creature he had seen sitting in the Strathers' office. The damn thing was a lot more awake tonight, and it looked pissed off as hell, since the crowd of spectators had been taunting the meat-eater for nearly an hour. It clawed up at the air with its huge paws spread wide, the needlelike claws coming out a good six inches, ready to rip the guts of anything that came near it. It was both a beautiful and fearsome beast, a big male, weighing, Stone estimated, a good six hundred pounds plus. Its teeth glistened in the sharp, dancing light of the flames, like daggers snapping open and shut, open and shut, the king roaring out his displeasure at having to deal with such fools.

Stone suddenly realized he had Excaliber with him, and a bolt of adrenaline braced through him as he expected to be pulled forward. But when he glanced down, he saw that the pitbull was as hypnotized by the sight as him. It was set in its hunting point, the tip of its nose lining up with its back, and a low growl escaped from its throat like the purr of a tank motor. But it didn't jump. It wouldn't voluntarily jump —not into that.

Suddenly there were cheers on the far side as Bronson came to the front of his people, leading three dogs. He led them right up to the side, pulling back hard on the heavily muzzled beasts. They were huge—mastiffs—just about the biggest canines Stone had ever seen, with thick, muscular bodies and jaws the size of paper cutters. They stared down at the lion, and all three pulled forward, wanting to jump into the fray, wanting to take on the tough boy. It took all of Bronson's rippling strength to hold them back.

"So you're giving me ten-to-one odds, right, Jayson Strather?" the biker leader screamed across the pit. "My three dogs against your toothless old fart of a lion here." He laughed loud, and his crew joined in.

"That's biting it on the balls, Bronson," the thin, ratlike face yelled back in that taunting, effeminate voice he seemed to use more and more the drunker he got. "If your dogs last even ten seconds, I'll be surprised."

"All right, then," Bronson bellowed. "I'm betting a thousand." He motioned for a biker behind him to come forward, pushing a wheelbarrow with two overstuffed burlap sacks. "Silver dollars every one of them." The biker sneered, kicking out his foot sideways so he hit into the side of a bag of silver, which hardly budged an inch. "Can you match it, asshole?"

"Match it." Jayson mock yawned, putting his powdered hand over his face as his brothers laughed. "A thousand is doughnut money for us, dearie, what I spend on makeup in a week. Please, please, I'm becoming drastically bored." He stuffed a whole fingerful of white powder into each nostril and sucked in hard, getting a strange smile on his face.

"Bored?" Bronson screamed. "Bored?" He ripped the muzzles from the three mastiffs and kicked them right in the asses, sending the animals over the side and into the pit. The fight was on so fast and moved with such rapidity that Stone could hardly follow it. But somehow he did, as if following a movie that suddenly jumped to ten times its regular speed, his eyes darting around the pit. The first dog that came down landed right atop the lion, which was the dog's bad luck, for the beast was waiting and ready. Rearing up on its hind legs, it caught the flailing canine with both huge front paws. It batted the dog back and forth what seemed like three or four times, incredibly fast, and then just threw the bloody thing to the side for later inspection.

The second dog must have thought he was a lion, for he landed right in front of the beast, just as it turned from disposing of the first. The mastiff opened its jaws, the saliva dripping down in a waterfall, its eyes wide with fear and the instinct to kill, the only task for which it had been trained. It suddenly leapt forward and caught the lion on the throat. But unfortunately for the dog, the mane was far too thick for its teeth even to inflict a flesh wound. And the lion didn't give it a second chance. It snapped its whole body out and up, sending the dog flying off it. Before the mastiff could launch another attack, the lion was on it, grabbing the creature by the head, crushing its whole skull in a great gush of blood like a white shark had just hit it. Taking a second crunch just for good measure, the lion tossed the dog back and forth in the air like a bloody towel, snapping every bone in the animal's body until its vertebrae must have been cracked in a thousand places.

Satisfied with the dog's dishrag status, the huge beast, its saucer-sized eyes glowing red and orange from the flames of the torches, turned to take on the third animal. But this one wasn't quite ready for the long haul. It had seen what the animal had done to its two buddies, and its enthusiasm for the fight had diminished considerably. The lion came toward it as the mastiff scrambled at the dirt walls of the pit, trying desperately to climb right up the sides. The lion suddenly charged in and swatted hard at the dog, with an uppercutlike motion of its front paw. Whether it intended to or not, the force of the blow that struck the mastiff at the same instant it was leaping up from the dirt sent the canine rocketing up into the air a good fifteen feet. Somehow it caught hold of the dirt sides of the pit, scampering like a paddle wheel on overdrive as its legs struggled to get a foothold. Which it did. And once up on terra firma, it took off through the crowd at full speed, headed for less exciting parts and less dangerous vocations.

"Bastard, bastard," Bronson was muttering from across the pit.

"Looks like I won, darling," Jayson screeched. "Do go collect my winnings, will you?" He addressed one of the thugs who constantly hovered around him. The man walked over to the wheelbarrow and started dragging the two loads of silver back.

"They was cowards, that's what," Bronson screamed, as if he'd been betrayed by the dogs. "They couldn't rise to the fuckin' occasion. They weren't champions, they were fakes. But there's more. I know where there's dogs that'll chew those up for dinner and take your pussycat down there and spit him out too. Hold on to my money, assholes. Don't you spend none of it." With that, the biker leader turned angrily and walked off, his people following right behind. The far side of the pit was empty within seconds as the whole gang disappeared off into the darkness and their motorcycles.

As the underling carried the money over to the Strathers brothers, who wiped their hands together eagerly, he got a little too close to the edge of the pit and misjudged a step. It's amazing how little it takes to die. For the weight of the silver dollars in his arms pulled him straight over, without a chance to recover. He screamed hard on the way down, realizing just where he was heading. The lion, which had gone over and begun chewing on the dead mastiff's heart—the first thing any gourmet lion goes for—heard the falling gang member behind it. It turned, this time slowly, seeing by the way the thing squirmed around the dirt floor that it couldn't move fast, couldn't fight, couldn't do anything.

"Should I shoot him, boss," one of the men at the edge of the pit screamed out to Jayson as he pulled out a submachine gun and lined up the stalking beast below, which was just inches from the man now.

"Kill my lion over some asshole who was clumsy enough to fall in? Hardly." Jayson laughed. "Besides, Pussy deserves a reward. Pussy did well in the fight. Shoot and you're a dead man." As the gangers around the pit looked on in horror at the man who had been one of their own, the lion leapt on him and caught the man's head in his huge, spreading jaws. It crunched hard as the Strathers minion continued to scream but couldn't quite break through, like a coconut shell that was just too hard. Then it bit a little harder, and the skull started to crack so that they could all hear it start to go. Brain fluids and slime suddenly poured out around the screaming man's face in a gush of hot tissue.

The lion crunched hard again, and this time it broke through. Like a walnut suddenly being squeezed by a nutcracker, the whole head exploded, the bone shattering in all directions, pieces of hair still attached. The entire brain itself, still throbbing inside, was exposed like a slug in a broken shell. The lion, holding the body up with both paws like a child playing with a doll, looked down at the glistening, undulating pink delicacy and opened its mouth. It swallowed the brain down whole with its long, sandpaperlike tongue, like a Wall Street exec taking down an oyster on the half shell as he rushed to catch the 4:45 to Hartford. The lion looked down into the hollow head to see whether there was any more of the delicious-tasting stuff and let out a whine of displeasure when it saw none. Knocking the brainless corpse down to the dirt, it began ripping open the stomach, and all the goodies that were contained there poured out. The dogs would be dessert.

"When he's full, sedate him and bring him back to the office," Jayson commanded his animal handlers as the other brothers rose with distinct expressions of happiness on their twisted faces. "And please, *do* wash off the money before you put it into the basement vaults. Blood *does* mess things up so."

Stone and Excaliber turned and headed off back to his room. They both looked shell-shocked, staring straight ahead, not even looking at each other. The pitbull had always prided itself on being afraid of nothing. And it hadn't been, until tonight. But the lion had scared the shit out of the animal and, because of that emotion—cowardice—it was filled with shame, the first time it had ever felt such a thing. But in its mind, as its fighting breed always did, it planned and visualized just how it would take out the carnivore—if it ever came after him.

Chapter
Seventeen _____

"**P**reacher Boy, you done real good yesterday," Vorstel said the next afternoon, his lips moving around his three twisted teeth in that prune of a mouth like he was trying to chew them down. The three brothers sat in their armchairs looking at Stone, who was in the "guest" chair about ten feet across the room. Vorstel, in particular, seemed all aglow about the contest. Stone's success at winning the trophy had reflected back on him and for the moment had added to his political power, his prestige over the other two. Since they were teens, they had all continually jockeyed for being topman, holding up people, ripping off cars, and then, after the collapse of what had been America, they found that their talents for ruthlessness, greed, and the ability to kill without mercy were excellent traits to possess in the new world. But as always, they trusted each other about as much as they trusted anyone else in this lying world. And Stone's trophy had complicated the already complex web of alliance and double dealings between them.

"Yes, you made me so proud yesterday," Jayson said, waving a sheer blue silk handkerchief back and forth in front

of his nose like a fan. He was heavily made up today, with
rouge on his cheeks and a purple-tinted lipstick. He was
fiddling with long false fingernails, gluing them on one by
one. They looked, actually, quite deadly, curving, Stone noticed, to sharp tips with steel points on them. The lion
chained by Jayson's side was sound asleep, its stomach still
distended after the meal of last night. Its face was dyed red
with blood, as were its claws. Stone wondered why his
throat always felt constricted when he was in this room, like
he wanted to just get up and run the hell out of there.

"So's we've decided to trust you," Rudolf said, his head
seeming to sink ever deeper into his neckless chest, "and
make you an official officer in our little thing here. Oh, we
ain't got sergeants, lieutenants, any of that shit. We got asshole, chief asshole, scumbag, top bag, and asskicker. We're
willing to make you an asskicker, Preacher Boy, an unpara-
lyzed opportunity."

"That's 'unparalleled opportunity,' you puke-brain," Jayson screamed loudly, fixing his brother with a cold stare.
"You do have to excuse my two brothers here," Jayson said,
addressing Stone dramatically, "they have the IQs of lower
life-forms. It is I who really run things. But let me translate
what the others are trying to say. We think you have the
makings of a topman. You follow orders, take care of some
nasty business, and the sky's the limit. That money you're
after, it's already here. See how quickly things come to those
who pray to Al?" He pointed over to the bag of silver dollars
that he had won from Bronson the night before. The lion
was using it to stretch one of its legs out on.

"Who do I have to kill?" Stone laughed harshly.

"A bunch of scum farmers about twenty miles from here.
The bastards have been meeting, organizing, trying to stop
paying us what's rightfully ours for protecting them from the
Head Stompers. We had to take out a bunch of 'em a few
days ago, but now we got word that the crazy sons of bitches
are going to try again. They're going to meet tonight. We
got someone on the inside—one of their top leaders—so we
know their every move. Where the meeting will be, when,

everything." Jayson reached over and scratched the lion with the steel-tipped fingernails of his right hand, digging into the mane. The huge beast let out with a purr that sounded like a diesel truck getting ready to shift into high gear.

"Sure," Stone said, squinting over at the lion, which had opened one eye and was looking straight at him like maybe it was starting to build up an appetite again. "Sounds like fun. A hell of a lot of fun."

"Excellent, excellent," Jayson exclaimed, sitting up straight and clapping his hands together. The other brothers smiled broadly—at least that's what Stone thought they were doing—but everything was so mangled up on the big mugs that it was hard to tell just what the hell was going on there.

"You'll lead a six man enforcer team," Vorstel said, cutting in on Jayson and giving him a dirty look. "You run the show top to bottom. Take out everyone and anyone you have to, whether it's one or fifty. We gotta stop this damn thing in the fucking bud." The brothers all looked at him, intently trying to see past his poker face. But Stone just smiled back greedily and glanced over at the sack of loot.

"For a bag of silver that fucking big, I'd strangle my own mother."

That night seven heavily armed men crawled through the darkness on the outskirts of the Hernandez farm, a scraggly, two-acre stretch that the brothers had given Stone the directions to. Hernandez was the one who'd come to Undertaker's place when Stone had been there. So it was coming full circle already, Stone mused as he moved through the darkness in the lead of the death squad. His plans were moving faster than he had figured, taking off, hitting rocket speed. He prayed he could hang on.

They had taken a beat-up old Ford station wagon with ancient, fake wood paneling on the side scrawled with graffiti about what the Head Stompers ate, did, and fucked. They parked the coughing vehicle about a mile from the place and then headed in with shotguns, subs, .45s, even a few grenades. Everything a man might need to create a mass slaughter of little old farmers who would be meeting inside a horse shed. The six killers treated Stone with respect. They had seen his shooting ability the day before. He was clearly someone not to fuck with.

They came up to the shed through some woods until they could see the flickering lanterns inside, a number of voices trying to talk softly. Stone gathered the Strathers' assassins around him.

"You three," Stone said, motioning to the men to the right of him, "will take to the right flank. I see a door there. You three take the left, through the window. I'll come in the front."

"Will do," the voices hissed back in the semidarkness, the half-moon above shimmering down through the pink-tinged radioactive stratosphere high above, giving a violet kind of glow to the proceedings. They moved forward in a crouch, the men readying their respective guns, and moved up to the two corners of the building. Inside, they could see men arguing now, an occasional voice rising in curses. Stone stood up as both groups of assassins got in place each about twenty feet away from him on opposite sides. They stared back toward him, waiting for his signal.

Suddenly Stone raised both of his weapons—the Ruger .44 and the mini-Uzi. Pointing one at each flank, he pulled the trigger and kept pulling. The bastards didn't know what hit them as the slugs poured into them. Within seconds it was all over, and six steaming bodies lay sprawled over one another, their own weapons untouched. Stone suddenly saw movement from one of the bodies, then heard a sharp retort. He felt a slug graze his upper left arm and winced in pain but instantly fired back with the few remaining shells in the Uzi. The ganger bounced around amid his red-coated fellows as Stone's bullets found their mark. Then he was still. All of them were still.

As Stone quickly reloaded his equalizer—just in case— the farmers who had been meeting inside came streaming out of every door. They started to run toward the hills until Hernandez, whose place it was, saw that the man with the guns was Stone. He stopped, and slowly, cautiously, the others walked back, forming a crowd around the fallen killers.

"You were all almost dead meat," Stone said, slapping the Redhawk and the auto back into their close-fitting holsters against his body. "These scum were sent to kill you." The farmers, now about a hundred strong, looked down at what they had almost been turned into, and their brown faces turned a lot whiter.

"We were meeting to figure out a way to—" Hernandez began, standing a few feet from Stone, his big straw farmer's hat in his trembling brown hands.

"Forget that organization stuff," Stone said sharply. "You've run out of time. The brothers want you all out of the picture. You understand what that means? Kaput, vamoose, fini. . . . You've got to fight back—and hard. Take the weapons of these dead gunmen, then hide, 'cause they'll send out more men. But listen, I'm with you, that's all I can tell you. I have a plan, an idea to set the two gangs against each other. But it's not quite time yet. I need another day or two. I'll need your help then. You understand me?" He looked around, addressing all of them, wanting every man to feel the intensity of his words.

"You can no longer be wimp farmers, poor little peasants who are being mistreated, and isn't it all so sad? I'm telling you if you don't fight back now—and with your blood— you will all be exterminated within the week. It's your choice, friends. I can't do any more." The farmers looked at one another, picked up the weapons of the fallen Strathers killers, and looked at them curiously.

"Practice with them," Stone said to Hernandez, who had lifted a big Army-issue nickel-plated .45. "But don't waste any ammunition. There's a shitload of guns in that town."

"We hear your words, Mr. Stone," Hernandez said, looking at the man who had just saved them all with a profound mixture of sadness and hope in his ancient eyes. "We will fight. We will arm ourselves with these—and with hoes and knives and sticks if we have to. But there is no turning back now. It is like you say. There but for your guns lie our bleeding bodies."

"Good, good," Stone said, looking sharply at the man. "But there's one more thing. One of you is a traitor." There was an audible gasp from the crowd. And voices yelled out, "No, no," in anger at Stone, an emotion he took as a good sign, as it meant they could feel rage as well as self-pity. And they would need a hell of a lot of that emotion to have the slightest chance of winning.

"Who?" Hernandez asked Stone without hesitation, knowing that if the man spoke the words, they were true.

"I don't know for sure. The brothers referred to him as someone on the inside, at the highest levels of the organization. Someone 'they would never suspect.'" The farmers looked around at each other suspiciously, a sudden wall of paranoia between them. Men they had trusted for years, decades, suddenly might be hated enemies. It gave them all a sick feeling in their guts, and tightly drawn faces as well.

Hernandez looked around at the group of five men who were standing closest to him, the leaders of the farmer's movement, and studied one of them closely, his eyes narrowing as if he were examining a frog pinned to a dissecting table.

"Miguel," he said suddenly, "come here." A young, handsome man with long wavy black hair stepped forward. He sported a long twirling mustache and the lusty, full-cheeked face that bespoke someone who knew how to have a good time, drink, love the ladies.

"Miguel, did you have anything to do with this?" Hernandez asked him as the man walked up to him and stepped about a yard away.

"Uncle, on my mother's grave, I swear I had absolutely nothing to do with any of this. Why, the very idea that you would even suspect—"

"Shut up," Hernandez snapped, his face growing colder and harder, like a body of water freezing up. "I've had my eye on you for months now, nephew. While the rest of us suffer, go around with sunken cheeks, you always seem to be well fed and have a self-satisfied air about you."

"Uncle, is it my fault that I love life, that I—" The man stuttered as he felt the eyes of a hundred other men on him.

"Empty your pockets," Hernandez said softly, but clearly enough for every man there to hear.

"What?" Miguel asked with a little laugh, as if he hadn't heard.

"You heard me, nephew, I know that your ears, along with all your other bodily organs, are in full functioning order. Empty your pockets." Miguel slowly reached down toward his pants pocket and extricated what was inside. As he lifted his hand out, his face seemed to drain of all color, his lips suddenly as dry as sand. For in the hand were ten silver dollars, perfect and glistening.

"Now—I—I can explain," Miguel began, looking at his uncle, at the others, his head turning back and forth. "I did some work for a man in town, helping him with painting and—"

"Nephew, I will use these dollars and whatever else I find on you to feed your widowed wife and your orphaned children."

"My widowed wife—" Miguel said, backing off, a look of sheer horror on his face. Suddenly there was a loud pop, and the .45 in Hernandez's hands burped with smoke. Miguel was sent flying backward as the slug entered his chest and quickly found his heart. He slammed down on his back, dead before he hit the dirt. He had no more excuses—and no need of them, either.

Chapter Eighteen _____

S tone burst into the Strathers brothers' headquarters like
a man who looked like he should be dead. He had
borrowed a little blood from the dead hit squad—they
had plenty and didn't seem to mind giving up a little—and
had smeared it all over his shoulder and leg, making him
look like he had just been through the Battle of the Bulge.

"W-what the hell?" Jayson stuttered as he saw the staggering Stone walk in, dripping little red drops on the floor
behind him.

"Ambush," Stone said in a breathless whisper, as if he
could hardly scrape up the energy for the words. "Your dou-
ble-dealer on the inside with the farmers must have been a
triple-dealer," he said bitterly. "The Head Stompers were
waiting for us before we even got to the goddamn farm." He
pulled out the small piece of chain that he had found on the
street the day before when the bikers had been in town and
threw it down on the floor at the brothers' feet.

"Man, it was a slaughter. I'll tell you, your boys fought
tough. Went out like men," Stone said, shaking his head in
appreciation. "But we didn't have a chance. I was lucky
even to get—" His right leg seem to buckle a little, and

Vorstel jumped up from the couch where he had been playing around with a newly arrived twelve-year-old whose body and face hadn't yet been mashed in by life in one of their whorehouses but soon would be.

"Here, sit down, Preacher Boy," the prune-mouthed giant said. "I'll get the doc."

"No, no," Stone protested, waving his hands. "It looks worse than it is. Caught two, maybe three slugs, but I think they're all flesh and muscle wounds, so I'll make it. The main thing is revenge," Stone said, sitting up straight, as if the mere thought of it gave him renewed energy.

"Goddamn right," Rudolf said, slamming his fist down so hard on the desk at which he sat that a crack appeared along the center and spread all the way across. "This is it, man," the neckless wonder said, looking back and forth at his two siblings. "We knew de day was going to come when de bastards was going to start trying to pick us off. It's wartime. War."

"Oh, do calm down," Jayson said, sitting cross-legged on a satin love seat along one wall as he filed away at his long nails, getting them just right. "War is hardly called for. Why should we lose a lot of our men and waste our money? There's easier ways to strike back."

"Like what?" Vorstel asked as he paced around the room looking like a caged grizzly ready to break out.

"Like, we snatch his son, his heir. The little bastard's only about eight or nine. I saw him yesterday riding behind his father when they came in. He keeps the squirt under guard so no one can get close to him. But *we* could get him. I'm sure. And once we had him—"

"Yeah, I like it." Vorstel nodded, and Rudolf grunted in assent, though the war idea was a lot more to his liking.

"Once we have his kid," Jayson said, twirling a silk scarf in front of him like a fan dancer, "we can dictate things around here. We'll have his balls in a bear trap."

"But maybe he doesn't care about the kid," Stone spoke up, starting to see his attempted manipulations to set the two gangs at each other's throats not quite heading in the direction he had hoped. "Maybe he'll just let him die."

"No way," Jayson said with a shrieking little laugh. "The bald-headed coot worships that little fucker. He wants to pass his whole operation on to the bald brat and start a fucking empire, to become Attila the Hun II. That kid's worth more to Bronson than his whole damn gang—guaranteed."

"But—" Stone spoke up.

"Hey, Preacher Boy, cool it," Jayson said, sounding annoyed. "You're just a hired hand, okay? We make the decisions around here. Now off to the doctor with you," he said suddenly, with a bizarre laugh. "Can't have our best hired gun all bloody, now can we?"

"But—" Stone tried to interject again.

"You!" Jayson said, addressing one of two guards who stood facing each other at the door to the room. "Take Preacher Boy here over to Doc's. Tell him top-of-the-line treatment for our boy, here." Stone saw that he was caught. There wasn't a goddamn thing he could do. His plans were veering off in a very unpredictable fashion.

"I get the money, right?" Stone suddenly piped up, realizing it would be out of character if he didn't demand it.

The brothers looked at each other for a few seconds. Then Jayson looked back at the blood-covered man.

"Sure you do, Preacher Boy, every penny of it. Though we'll have more work for you soon—lots of it, I'm sure."

"All right, then," Stone said, rising as one of the guards grunted and pointed the direction. As Stone turned and walked out, the three brothers gathered in the center of the room talking and gesticulating wildly as they planned the abduction of the biker child. The guard led Stone across the street and down about three blocks, through a seedy-looking bar and into the back where he pounded hard on a metal door that wasn't set quite right on its hinges.

"Doc, Doc, open up, you son of a bitch," the man screamed, and after about ten seconds the door creaked open. Stone looked in and down at the bloated red face of a longtime alkie. The fat face looked positively diseased:

pores all enlarged on his cheeks; huge nose with broken blood vessels like red spiderwebs all over it; great cauliflower ears, half eaten away, that sat on each side of the alcohol-twisted face.

"Yeah, what the hell you want?" the man asked, and Stone could see a bottle of liquor poking out of the filthy gray bloodstained smock he wore. The doctor squinted through thick bifocals, one lens cracked down the middle, at his unwelcome visitors. "Christ, man, it's past midnight. Can't a man drink in peace in this goddamn town anymore?"

"Oh, shut your drunken face, you old alkie." The guard sneered with disgust. "Here, this stupid fool will see to your wounds," the Strather man said with a harsh laugh, and walked off, praying that he'd never be hurt bad enough to need to be treated by the likes of that. The brothers had had him on payroll for years now, needing some kind of medical man around, since their own employees tended to get shot up or knifed now and again. The sixty-year-old M.D., who had been kicked out of three medical schools but who had at least once been a credible doctor, was now hardly capable of spreading butter on bread. Still, old habits die hard. So the man stayed on, lost in drunken reminiscences of a past that had never existed.

"Well, come on in, I suppose," the doctor said, grabbing Stone's wrist with a limp grip and pulling him in. "Close the door, don't let the pollen in. Come on." He led Stone past the anteroom, filled with old magazines and newspapers strewn all over the place like a tornado had just whipped through, then into a second room where medical equipment, most of it rusting and broken, lay in heaps and disorganized piles all over the place.

"Here, sit here, right here," Doc said, patting a steel table. He pulled out a piece of the sanitary paper that doctors traditionally use, only this piece was being reused and was coated with dried slime and blood from previous patients.

"Ah, look, Doc, I really don't think it's so bad," Stone said, not wanting the bastard to get a close look at his "wounds."

"Nonsense, nonsense," the doctor said, pushing him more firmly now, so he had to step backward and ended up sitting on the table. "Everyone who's sent by the brothers has to undergo an exam. It's the rules, mister." He pulled the bottle from his smock pocket, took a deep guzzle, his huge, stubbly Adam's apple bobbing up and down four times before he stopped. "And rules is rules." He giggled, his eyes spinning around like pennies caught in a washing machine. "Want some?" He held out the bottle, which Stone could see was the brown stuff—not his favorite.

"I'll pass," Stone replied, holding up his hand with a highly depressed look on his face. He glanced over to a second table in the half darkness of the candlelit room, and his face winced in horror. For the good doctor had already been working on someone else—only this one was already dead. A corpse. And God only knew what he had been doing—the damn thing was cut up all which ways, its pieces lying like unassembled parts to a huge cut-and-paste doll, arms lying alongside legs, the eyes and ears all cut from the face, and stacked neatly in little piles.

"Jesus, God," Stone mumbled silently in prayer deep inside himself. Just being in the place and around the red-faced wino doctor gave him the creeps.

"Now, let me just take a look at your injuries here, my good man," the doctor said, capping the bottle and slamming it back in his pocket. He stepped in real close, so Stone had to smell his stinking alcohol and cigar-saturated breath and look into his red-pored, exploded-capillary face and try not to vomit. The doc looked around the areas on which Stone had splashed blood and poked and prodded with his fingers, trying to find the entry holes. After about sixty seconds he stopped and stepped back about a yard so he was staring right into Stone's face.

"You're not wounded, you lying bastard. What the hell's going on here?"

"Shit." Stone grimaced, starting to reach for his gun, knowing his cover had been blown and instantly trying to start computing what that meant. But suddenly the Doc's hand moved real fast. A scalpel he kept concealed just inside the sleeve of his smock on the right hand came darting up. Before Stone could even respond—as he was totally unprepared—the glistening scalpel slammed into his shoulder, coming straight down.

"Fuck," Stone screamed out, grabbing the man's hand and twisting it so that the doctor turned beet-red with pain from the jujitsu hold as he was bent over backward, nearly halfway to the ground. "I thought doctors were supposed to heal, not stab," Stone said angrily as he reached over with the free hand and pulled out the blade. It stung like fire as he extracted it, and a stream of blood ran down his chest and back from the wound.

The doctor was sputtering away, trying to rise, but the hold that Stone had on him was unbreakable. "What the hell am I going to do with you, you old fart?" Stone asked as he looked quickly around the room. "I really should kill you. But there's something so pathetic about you, I don't think I could stand the memory of that red nose on my conscience forever. So—"

He pushed the man around the room, as if guiding a wheelbarrow with one hand, and the doctor sputtered and wheezed and bumped into things as he stumbled along. Stone saw some twine and surgical tape and reached for them. He suddenly kicked around, catching the ankle of the doctor, knocking him straight to the ground so that the man fell on his face, knocking a trio of teeth free in a bloody little clump.

"I'm just going to tie you up," Stone said, wrapping Doc's wrists and feet together in an unbreakable knot his father had taught him, one that would only get tighter the more a man struggled. "You ain't going to die unless you struggle and have a heart attack, which would be fine with me. Up to you." He slammed some surgical tape over the still sputtering doctor, who was having trouble even getting a few words together. Stone dragged the man by his ankles along the filthy, bloodstained floor with dried pieces of human anatomy from other "autopsies" lying around the place like

droppings from a picnic of ghouls. Mice and rats poked
through them here and there, carrying off unrecognizable,
dark, shriveled things back to their holes to eat them away
from their greedy kin.

"Here, Doc," Stone grunted as he half pushed, half kicked
the big body of the alkie doctor into a closet. "Thanks for
the treatment—I'll tell all my friends to come here for every
little injury." He slammed the door shut and walked quickly
out of the chamber of horrors. But the shit was about to hit
the fan, of that there was no fucking doubt. He'd have to get
the hell out of town, fight from the outside. It was too bad.
But there was no getting around it. His cover was as blown
as the *Hindenburg*.

Stone walked outside, looking around carefully to make
sure no one was keeping an untoward eye on him. But as far
as he could tell, there were just a few drunken stragglers
heading back to their filthy little rooms somewhere to sleep
it off. He shifted his hip holster and pulled his jacket back
slightly so he could have quick access. Somehow he had a
feeling he was going to need it. He'd get the dog and then
get the fuck out of there.

As he slipped back to the whorehouse through the back
alleys rather than the main streets, every dark window he
passed seemed menacing, as if barrels were poking from
every sill. It was that doctor, that's all, Stone told himself.
The murderous old bastard had set him completely edge, just
having to touch that bloated flesh. . . .

He reached the whorehouse by going over a few fences
and came in through one of the back screen doors. He entered a room filled with supplies for the house—buckets,
mops, a stack of wood for the winter—and started forward
into the dimly lit hallway. Suddenly there was a motion to
his right, and a shape leapt forward, slamming an ax handle
down on his head. Stone parried the blow at the last fraction
of a second, taking a hard strike on his forearm, but stopping
the handle from reaching his head. As he started forward, to
throw a smashing blow to his attacker's face, he sensed

movement again right behind him. And even as the baseball bat descended on the back of his head, his father's admonition, "Where there's one, there's two," echoed around in his head like a record stuck in its groove.

Chapter Nineteen _____

The first thing he heard when he came to were angels singing. Only they were singing off-key, and as he came out of the painful blackness, Stone saw that they weren't angels at all, and they weren't singing. It was one of the Strathers brothers—Vorstel—and he was looking down at Stone from above, as if he were just about the funniest damn thing Vorstel had ever seen in all his days. Stone tried to move and found that his wrists and legs were completely immobilized. He was strapped down.

"You fucked up, didn't you, Preacher Boy?" Vorstel sneered, his three-toothed mouth twisting around like the face of some nightmarish eel at the bottom of the sea. "You almost got away with it, asshole, except for one thing. Jayson saw you pick up that piece of chain yesterday. He figured you was saving it for a memento. But you wasn't, was you? You was planning to double-cross us." His fist suddenly slammed down, and Stone's head rocketed around on his body like it was thinking about flying off on vacation somewhere.

"That's for lying," Vorstel said, glaring down, his smile now changed to something else, something twisted. "And this"—he grinned, cocking the fist again so that it looked like it was as big as a sledgehammer—"is for making an asshole out of me in front of my brothers, since I brought you into our thing." The knuckle meteor came straight down into the side of Stone's head, and again his consciousness went on and off, like a light bulb flickering from a shorting wire.

Then Stone heard a scream that was even louder than the explosions in his skull, and the blurred shadow above him suddenly disappeared.

"Hey, don't start without me, you bastard," Vorstel yelled, and Stone heard him take about six steps, his boots slamming hard on the concrete floor. He heard what sounded like the droning whir of a piece of machinery, and then another scream, this one much shriller and more drawn-out than the previous one. In fact, it didn't stop. Somehow Stone raised his head, which wasn't tied down, and saw Vorstel and his brother, Rudolf, in front of a large metal device about fifteen feet away. It must have been some kind of press, for a huge, flat, square section about five feet by five feet was being lowered down onto another similarly shaped section. Only someone's arm was being held inside the thing. And it was just a kid.

Bronson's son, Stone realized in a flash, as his brain cells returned to a state of semi-functioning inside his battered skull. The bastards had put the kid's hand inside an ancient paper press, and it was coming down a fraction of an inch at a time onto the hand, which was tied around the wrist to the edge of the thing.

"Let *me* turn that damn contraption," Vorstel exclaimed loudly, his voice echoing off the stark concrete walls of what Stone assumed to be the brothers' torture chamber, since there were various other tables around, and a man, maybe dead, sitting half propped up against a wall at the far side of the room.

"Oh, here you go, for chrissake," Rudolf said, standing back and letting his sibling have a go at the wheel, which was attached to a pulley system that slowly brought the flat press down. He looked over at the eight-year-old boy's face as if enjoying seeing the pain on it, pain caused by him as he turned the wheel. The son of Bronson was trying to act brave. He looked like a miniature version of his old man, bald head, tattoo on each side of his skull, wearing leather pants and vest with studs. But still, he was just a boy, and as the press slowly came down and crushed his bones and flesh and muscle all together into a sludge of red, the lad let out with the most unearthly sound that Stone had ever heard.

"Now, my turn on the other hand," Rudolf demanded, pushing Vorstel out of the way. "You can't hog the damn press for every fucking part of him." Vorstel turned around for a second to look at Stone, who was watching the scene with a sickened expression, as the press was slowly raised back up again about a foot above the smashed hand, and a whole flood of ooze and slime dripped down over the side of the rusting metal and onto the floor. There was nothing left of the hand at all—just the crushed stump of the lad's wrist, which ended at the very base of what had been the hand. The boy looked down at it, his eyes wide, as if they'd just seen God. He couldn't even scream—his mouth just hung open, his tongue sort of moving around inside like a worm trying to get off a fishhook.

"Ain't that something," Vorstel yelled over when he saw Stone watching. "Just got it last week. Ain't had a chance to test it out. But it works fine, works just fine. And Mr. who-ever-the-hell-you-are"—Vorstel sneered, his heavily lidded eyes narrowing—"after we crush this little fucker, crush every little bit of him into Jell-O, then we're going to start on you, friend. And I'll just let you wonder where we're going to start first." With that, he turned back to see just what the hell was going on, as he didn't want to miss a bit of the action. Rudolf had tied the boy's other hand to the side of the press and was pushing it in with one hand while he turned the wheel that lowered the top slab of metal with the other. The boy watched as the press came down, watched as his eyes grew bigger and bigger, his pulp of a right hand hanging limply at his side, sending a little waterfall of red and pink down onto the floor.

Stone knew he had minutes, maybe seconds, to live. Once the boy was either squashed or dead—whichever came first —they would vent their sadistic madness on him. And he knew one thing—that though he didn't mind dying, he didn't want to go out like that. Please, God, not like what they were doing to that poor little murderous son of a bitch over there. He searched desperately through his mental bag of tricks as he tested his bindings, pulling hard, but with hardly any motion so as not to catch their attention, though there wasn't much danger of that as the blood perverts were firmly rooted in what was gong on in front of them.

His left wrist was slightly loose. Not much, but there was just enough slack so that when he turned it, he could feel that he could almost slip under the leather binding. Stone twisted and pulled at the damn thing like a snake caught in a trap, trying to free himself. Slowly, agonizingly slowly, for every second seemed like an hour as he heard the boy's screams start up again when the press started to squeeze against his right hand.

Stone's arm suddenly snapped free of the bindings at the exact second that Vorstel just happened to glance over to see how his honored guest was doing.

"Motherfucker," he screamed, "he's getting out, he's getting out." They stopped what they were doing, leaving the press just as it was starting to crush the bones below, and came roaring over toward Stone, pulling huge hunting knives from inside their jackets.

"Son of a fucking—" Stone snarled to himself as he reached down toward his boot, straining with every sinew to get to the push dagger hidden inside the heel of his right boot. At least it would give him a weapon, as Stone saw that his pistols had been stripped from him. But he wasn't going to get the chance, for the two brothers were tearing ass toward him like they were in the hundred-yard dash. With a push of breath to relax himself, Stone suddenly shifted his whole body and pulled the entire table he was on right over

on its side. The thing crashed with a great roar, as it was
made of steel, and Stone felt himself jarred hard as he hit
shoulder and hip first onto the concrete floor.

But it brought him a few seconds of precious time as the
brothers slammed into the legs of the thing and got tangled
up in the mess, the table creating a momentary obstacle.
Stone reached down for the boot, struggling hard, as it was
just beyond his reach at the half-crunched angle he was lying
in, with half the weight of the table on him. Then somehow
he reached his boot and pushed the heel hard to the right,
catching the three-inch-long blade as it fell into his hand. He
fitted the small knife in his palm and gripped his fingers over
the hilt. It was designed with the blade coming out of the
middle of the handle and pointing straight out, perpendicular
from it. Thus the user could grip his whole hand around the
handle and have the knife blade project forward right between his fingers. It was a commando ace-in-the-hole, just
one of the Major's many little "last-resort" tricks. It certainly
qualified for that category.

Stone pulled himself out straight again and slashed at the
binding of the other hand, which cut loose with a single
slice. Then he leaned forward again and freed his right foot.
But time was running out—he could hear them rising, un-
tangling themselves, coming around each side of the table.
He was reaching to cut the final binding when Vorstel appeared from the left, his face snarling like a dog with rabies,
foam and whatnot bubbling out from his enraged lips. He
raised his immense hunting knife and started to bring it
down like a machete, but Stone lashed out with his free leg.
It was just a snap kick, not even that hard, but then they
didn't have to be when they were aimed right against the
opening of the kneecap. And this one was right on target.
The huge killer buckled and crashed to the ground like a safe
thrown from a second-story window.

Stone sliced at the binding, which took two cuts to sever.
He felt the shadow of Rudolf closing in on him from the left,
just as his leg pulled free. Stone didn't even try to block.
Instead, he moved in the direction of his body, which was

slightly facing forward, and somersaulted low to the ground. Rudolf's blade descended like an ax, slamming straight into the side of the table. So immense was his strength and momentum that the super-hardened steel blade bit right into the stainless-steel table for several inches with a shrill fingernail-on-blackboard kind of sound.

But Stone was gone—the somersault took him right over Vorstel, who was just starting to rise up onto one knee, lifting his knife again. Stone used the big ganger's back as a kind of ramp, and he rolled right over the top, coming down about two yards away against one of the concrete walls that ringed the basement chamber. He turned on a dime, and not too soon, since Vorstel had gotten up and was charging at him like a maddened bull. With a tilt of his head Stone dodged the knife blade that was thrust out suddenly. He stepped quickly to the right at a forty-five-degree angle, using the momentum of Vorstel's body to let it go slightly past him. Gripping the push dagger in his left hand, Stone went into boxing stance and jabbed out hard into the huge ganger's left rib cage.

The knife flew in and out like a jackhammer. Vorstel didn't even quite know what happened, though a little tremor of something ran across his face. As he turned to face Stone, he felt another stab of pain in his gut, then in the side of his arm. Stone just kept jabbing out, circling quickly around the man as he kept his eye on Rudolf, who was stuck for a few seconds trying to dislodge his knife, which he had embedded in the steel operating table. It was easier to get it in than to get it out.

Vorstel didn't know what the hell was happening. He was huge, a monster, had killed countless numbers of men, usually with one blow. But Stone was fast, and he wasn't about to fight the oversized killer's way. He fought in his own nasty style—it was called survival. So as Vorstel lunged wildly forward over and over again—it being the one method of fighting he had ever had to practice—Stone danced around the gang topman, snapping out the hand with the blade poking out from between his middle two fingers.

Again and again the knife ripped into flesh, then pulled out. All over Vorstel's body, big blotches of red were oozing through his clothes. He was a pincushion, one that bled.

Suddenly Stone saw the man's face cloud up for a second, as boxers do when they've taken a hard shot. Vorstel stopped for a moment, looked down at the butchered flesh that was his own body, and turned a ghostly shade of green. For he realized why he hurt—he hadn't even seen the blade in Stone's hand, just the fist snapping out. But now he saw it. And having killed so many, Vorstel knew just by the amount of blood streaming from him, from the number of stab wounds, that he was a dead man.

But Stone wasn't going to allow the dying man to call a priest. He saw his chance and took it. The instant he saw Vorstel look down and lose his concentration for a moment, Stone stepped right in front of the gang leader and ripped the blade across the man's throat. Right to left, then left to right. He stepped back as the throat exploded out in an avalanche of red, which splattered over the floor and Stone's boots and pants. Vorstel's knife fell from his fingers as he threw both hands over the throat, gripping it, as if trying to strangle himself. But as much as he tried to hold it all inside, like someone stuffing dirt under a rug, there was just a little too much junk pouring out of him. He staggered backward and slammed hard into the wall, cracking the back of his head, though it hardly mattered anymore.

"Cchh, yhhhhgghh!" He was clearly trying to say something as he stared right at Stone, but for the life of him, Stone couldn't understand what it was. Then he dropped to the floor in a sitting position, and his hands fell away from the throat, the lifeless eyes still focused on the man who had just killed him.

Stone heard a sudden sound and whipped around, holding the knife at ready. But he was too late—Rudolf was there, right in his face, the huge knife with the cracked bone handle coming in like an ICBM from hell. Stone knew in a fraction of an instant that he was a dead man. That he couldn't duck, move, dive, parry, or stab the bastard who was just a foot from his nose and coming at about ninety miles per hour. His whole body tensed up as it prepared to die. And then, though his father would have whipped his hide, Stone closed his eyes just for a second as the knife came right toward them.

He waited for the blow but felt nothing. Then he heard a wet thud and a gurgling sound. By the time his eyes opened, only a second later, Rudolf was already flying past. And embedded in his back was a round saber-saw blade a foot in diameter. The steel blade had penetrated the man's back, severed his spine like a piece of balsa wood, cut through his lungs, popping them like balloons, and then continued out through the front so that about ten of the jagged, inch-long cutting teeth poked out, like the jaws of some hideous larva eating its way from the inside out. The man kept running past Stone, as if he were late for his own funeral, and slammed headfirst into one of the concrete walls, smashing his face into bloody mashed potatoes. The whole mess just sort of slithered to the floor, where it lay all ripped and red like something ready for landfill.

Stone turned his head and saw the Bronson kid. He was standing about thirty feet away across the room and was holding his stump of a hand with an expression of raw pain dancing across his face. But the little fucker had clearly thrown the blade, one of the brothers' many toys lying around the room. The kid had thrown it all the way across the basement and managed to take out a killer whom a hundred other men hadn't been able to. And even in the midst of his agony, the kid managed a grim smile for Stone, as if to say, "We fucked these assholes up pretty bad, didn't we?"

Stone looked back across the vast distance of blood and savagery that separated him from the biker boy and whispered, "Yeah."

Chapter Twenty _____

Stone tourniqueted the kid's hideous stump. There wasn't a hell of a lot else he could do. The biker brat needed an operation at a hospital with a team of neuro-surgeons, which, since there were no functioning hospitals in the entire country, was an unlikely proposition to say the least. But once the main stream of blood was slowed so he at least knew the kid wouldn't bleed to death, Stone knew he couldn't do any more. He retrieved his pistols from where they were hanging on a wall and handed the kid one of the dead brothers' blood-splattered guns—a World War II Luger all scraped and bent like it had been through about ten wars. The kid seemed reluctant at first to accept the weapon. He had been trained in killing multiple opponents with knives, chains, blades, and tricks of every kind. But not guns. His biker clan used them only as a last resort. But after thinking about the fact that he had only one hand now—and wasn't feeling his greatest—the kid took it and gripped it hard.

Stone didn't know if the little bastard couldn't, or just wouldn't, speak, but he didn't utter a word to Stone. He just looked around furtively all the time. He seemed more animal than human, and Stone felt a strange revulsion for the muscle-bound eight-year-old miniature of his father's barrel-chested, tree-limbed physique.

"Come on," he said, motioning once he had his firearms strapped back on and loaded. Moving slowly, the barefoot kid behind him, clad only in black leather pants, Stone led the way to the back staircase. As far as he could determine, the main stairs were at the opposite end. There was just a chance that this was a service or emergency exit, because he knew there would be a shitload of guards in front of the place. Stone went up the stairs, taking from his pocket the push dagger, which was still soaked in red from the throat it had recently cut.

He pushed open the thick wooden door at the top a fraction of an inch at a time. They were in luck. It opened to a backyard filled with refuse and junk, and a chain-link fence about forty yards off, and then woods another hundred yards or so beyond. Glancing down, Stone saw that the biker kid, even though horribly wounded, had a look of anticipation on his slightly demonic face. He lived to fight, to kill, to let blood. His father had schooled him well.

Stone pushed open the door hard and saw, to his horror, a guard leaning back on a chair reading a dirty magazine. So engrossed was he in the size forty-fours staring up at him that he didn't catch the movement until Stone was upon him. Stone kicked out the legs of the chair at the same time he slammed his hand over the reader's forehead, pushing him straight back into the cement walk behind him. The back of the thug's skull cracked in twenty places, and the whole head seemed to cave in like an egg hit by a hammer. But Stone was gone by the time the body hit the ground. He and the boy shot across the yard filled with debris from the past —pieces of rusting cars, broken washing machines and refrigerators, all the things that had slowly disappeared from use since electricity and every appliance it had powered had also disappeared from the territory.

The kid was a little speed demon, pushing Stone to exert himself to his limits just because he couldn't stand the idea of being beaten by a fucking eight-year-old. Leaping wreckage, running right over jagged springs and piles of busted bricks, the two reached the link fence at exactly the same instant. They both kept their momentum going, pushing off with the last step so they landed two thirds of the way up the ten-foot-high fence. Then they were over and off into the field, filled with weeds and broken glass. Stone winced when he thought of the kid's feet going over the sharp edges, but apparently they were so callused, or the kid was so tough, that he ran on without the slightest faltering or expression of pain.

Then they were at the woods, and both stopped short and turned to see if they were being pursued. But they weren't. Stone turned to the junior biker and said, breathing hard, "Thanks kid."

The biker heir looked at Stone with that animal stare that he seemed to take on the whole world with, like some kind of wild child raised by the dogs or the wolves, then his mouth moved into a grimace, as if it were hard for him even to say the word.

"Thanks," he hissed out like a mountain cat. And suddenly he turned and was gone. Gone in a flash into the bushes and shadows of the forest. Stone turned and headed in the other direction, toward the whorehouse. He had to get the damn dog out of there. The bastards would take it out on Excaliber, of that Stone had no doubt. He carefully made his way to the brothel, through the ten blocks of alleys and side streets. As he turned the last corner he looked around, checking for the reflection of muzzles at the windows. They hadn't come here yet. Maybe they still didn't know he'd escaped.

But as Stone took one more step toward the place, some twenty yards off, he saw that he was completely and terribly wrong. They *did* know and they *were* waiting. Jayson flanked by a half dozen lower-echelon gangers, blocked his path. Yet Jayson and his thugs didn't particularly concern Stone. What concerned Martin Stone was the lion that Jayson was holding on a chain leash. The lion that was staring at Stone and licking its chops.

"I underestimated you from the start, Mr. Preacher Boy," the effeminate gang leader said. He was now dressed in some kind of lime-green toga that covered his body from neck to foot, and one of those omnipresent silk scarves that he wore wrapped around his neck and the lower part of his face. His thin cheeks were heavily rouged for the occasion, and dark purple lipstick outlined his mouth in a heart shape. "I knew you were tough, but I didn't realize you were smart too. But then you're not that smart or you wouldn't be standing there now, would you?" He laughed, a little chirp of disdain, and then reached down to unchain the lion.

"I really ought to thank you in a way. It's funny how things work out." Jayson grinned. "With my brothers dead, *I* run the show now. I always hated the dumb bastards, anyway. It's too bad you couldn't have stuck around. You and I would have made a great team." He blew Stone a kiss, then pulled the clasp back on the lion's chain. "But of course now I *have* to kill you." The lion looked around, confused for a moment, until Jayson pointed at Stone and said, "Kill him, Pussy. Rip his guts out."

The lion had taken but one step forward toward its target when they all heard a howling, smashing, growling, and breaking sound that was extremely loud. Even the lion stopped, startled, the mane on its neck going up like a porcupine. The whole crew looked up at the second story of the whorehouse where the unearthly sounds were coming from just in time to see an insane dog burst right through the window, sending the glass, frame, and all exploding out into the street. Excaliber landed on a small six- by five-foot terrace outside the windowsill, trailing a long chain that was pulling the entire brass bed behind it, one end of which had reached the wall at the window. The pitbull stared down at the scene below, instantly figuring out just what the hell was going on. Then it launched itself like a NASA rocket headed for the moon.

Everything exploded into violent motion. The chain of the dog reached its limits, and it became a question only of which was going to go first—the dog's thick, muscular neck or the tube of brass that the chain was attached to. But there

was no question, really. The brass vertical tube snapped
dead center, and both broken pieces flew out like projectiles
toward opposite walls. The pitbull took off right over the
small wall of the terrace and descended straight down toward the lion below, like a hawk swooping down from the
sky for a rabbit, not quite realizing that this particular rabbit
was three times as big as him and had teeth that belonged in
the Smithsonian.

The lion, realizing that the shit was hitting the fan, decided to carry out its order to kill Stone first—then it would
deal with this puny white thing hurtling toward it. It charged
forward, the ten yards toward Stone, coming at him with
blood in its eyes. But Stone had taken advantage of the momentary diversion of the pitbull's theatrics to pull out his
Ruger. As the lion was about to make its death leap, he got
off a shot. Stone missed the beast's head but took out its
right front leg, and it tumbled over in a spill as Stone dived
to the right to escape the momentum of the rolling body.
Before the animal could even rise, Excaliber had bolted up
onto its back. God knew just what the pitbull thought he was
doing—quite possibly the dog didn't quite know itself—but
it appeared that the dog was trying to ride the thing as if
leaving the gate at the Annual Canine Rodeo. The lion let
out with a brain-shattering roar as it wildly tried to dislodge
the insane flea clinging to its back.

But Stone didn't have time to watch what was going to
happen next, for the second that he got off the single shot
that nipped the lion's right leg, Jayson came charging at him
with a wild shriek like Tony Perkins in *Psycho*. Both of the
gang leader's hands suddenly emerged from out of his purple
toga, and the long, clawlike fingernails slashed at the air like
daggers. Stone was amazed at how fast the guy was. Somehow he had thought of the two dead brothers as the tough
ones, but this son of a bitch moved like a goddamn leopard.
He lunged and clawed and rushed at Stone, the six-inch-long
steel nails ripping at the air again and again like spiked paddle wheels digging for blood.

Stone stumbled as he tried to back out of the way. And

that was almost the last mistake *he* ever made, for Jayson was upon him in a flash. The skinny madman leapt toward Stone, slashing in a blur with his right hand. Stone felt a searing pain along his whole right side as the claws dug into his flesh about half an inch deep and a foot down. The sudden pain sent his Ruger flying from his hand as the fingers went completely numb. Somehow he managed to parry the second hand that he knew was coming. He got off a quick leg kick to the shin, and Jayson fell backward as Stone glanced down and saw that although blood was pouring from his side like it was cheap, he was going to live at least from *that* slice. But Jayson did a backward roll as he hit the ground and came up, instantly moving forward again. He let out a cheap imitation of the lion's roar, though in its own way, Stone found it no less frightening, and charged again.

Stone looked at the pistol lying on the ground about ten feet away, but there was no time. Off to the side he heard a dreadful sound, like something screaming horribly, and then he heard a great commotion. But there wasn't time to see what the hell was going on with the damn dog. For Jayson, again with amazing speed, was flying toward him, his lime-green toga whipping all around him, revealing bony white legs with injection marks running up and down, all cratered like the moon. The steel claws beelined for Stone's face, ready to rip out anything they touched. Jayson had eviscerated and killed many a tough, tough man with these claws. Stone was about to join the club.

But the would-be victim wasn't quite ready to be taken out by fake fingernails. As Jayson came in, Stone twisted suddenly around and to the side of him——an aikido move his father had taught him for avoidance of knives and bayonets. As the right claw came searching for him, Stone grabbed around the wrist and pulled hard, snapping his other hand over the top of Jayson's so he had the claw-hand trapped between his own. He turned his hip with a lightning snap, and Jayson stopped dead in his tracks and flipped right up into the air, making a circle above the ground with his wrist

as the center. As he came down, Stone positioned his own
hand just right, meeting the falling body.

With his right hand controlled by Stone, Jayson flew
down headfirst, right into his own curved steel fingernails.
The six-inch-long daggerlike claws dug into the center of his
face, and both eyes were pierced cleanly through, so that the
hand pushed all the way into Jayson's brain and exited out
the back. Stone jumped back, letting go of his attacker. It
was a horrible sight, a man impaled on his own hand. The
claws pierced through in five places, brain and slime issuing
out from every puncture. The brother's eyeballs, both of
them skewered like onions, slid out around the claws and
down onto his face.

Jayson stumbled backward, taking one little step after another, as if he were learning some new dance. He tried to
scream but could only get a pitiful little mewing sound to
come out from between his bloody lips. Then, pulling hard
with his other hand, he somehow ripped out the claw from
his face and it flew free. An explosion of all that was in his
head followed close behind, like baggage afraid it would
miss the plane. Brain tissue, blood, both eyeballs trailing
tendrils, and yolk sacks—all flew out, covering the front of
the body and sliding to the ground. Then the last of the
Strathers brothers collapsed in a pile of his own slime and
started to rot.

As Stone had been battling for his very life, Excaliber had
been doing the same. His ride aboard the lion had lasted all
of three seconds before the beast threw him off with a great
heave of its golden shoulders. The huge predator turned and
searched for the pitbull who, by instinct, had leapt off in a
different direction the moment he landed. He came in suddenly from the lion's right side, jaws open to the maximum,
not aware that dogs weren't supposed to fight lions. Not
unless the species had been bred for it, like his had. The lion
pushed forward to charge, but in trying to compensate for its
broken right leg, which Stone had shot, the creature went a
little too high as it leapt at the terrier.

And that was all that Excaliber needed. Seeing the opening, he changed his motion in mid-stride and, instead of going up, went sharply down. The lion's stretched jaws passed just overhead as they snapped closed on dogless air. Excaliber shot down low as he passed underneath the huge carnivore. Then, seeing an excellent target, he slammed his teeth down on the lion's testicles, which were right in front of him. Closing like a bear trap around them, the dog pulled hard and bit them free of the body, tossing them high in the air so that they shot up like tennis balls and didn't come down for a good forty feet.

The lion let out a roaring scream that sent crows flying from trees a mile off. It jumped and fell and writhed around in the dirt and seemed to go into quite an epileptic-type seizure. The pitbull was the *last* thing on its mind. Its fucking balls had been snipped off, and it wasn't going to get them back again. The carnivore rushed forward, jumping from side to side, out of control, as if electric currents were going through all its muscles. The huge jaws bayed to the cruel skies as it ran.

Mercifully for the animal, some of the Strathers gang, standing in a half circle around the street, thought the creature was coming at them and peppered it with a sudden barrage of fire, sending the thing skidding in a bloody pile right into two of the men, sending them flying. There it lay, its big eyes staring in dead shock at the emasculation it had suffered, a tragic ending for so noble a beast.

But the lion's death was the last thing Stone or the pitbull, which walked to his side with a murderous look in its burning eyes, had to worry about. Dozens of the Strathers gang were gathering on each side of them, coming down the street from both ends. And as they came, they took out their pistols, their knives, their brass knuckles, their ice picks. These two were going to be turned into Swiss cheese. The gang's leaders were dead, but their underlings still knew how to kill.

Chapter
Twenty-one _____

"**D**og, it's been nice," Stone said as he raised both pistols toward the approaching killers. "And thanks for that lion bit—that took balls." The pitbull looked at him and winced, as if offended by the pun. Then it turned toward the advancing ranks and picked out the closest of the gangers in its mind, deciding that he would be the first one it would strike. It knew the odds said it was all over. The dog was no fool.

Just as the gangers began closing in to strike the final blows, there was a commotion from an alley right across the street from Stone. And to his amazement and joy a whole fucking cavalry of farmers came riding in, with Hernandez in the lead. They rode mules and donkeys, horses and ponies. Some ran in bare feet. But they had come to fight, as Stone had told them they must. In their hands were machetes and hoes, pitchforks and shovels with both edges sharpened. They obviously didn't have a hell of a lot of firepower, but they had guts by the ton. Stone's tired face couldn't help but grin as he saw the jaws of the gang members drop open at the sight of an invasion of little brown farmers coming in on mangy mules moving at about eight miles per hour. It was hard for their slow minds to assimilate such information.

But the farmers were for real. And one of the Strathers gang, unlucky enough to be in the front ranks, found that out as a pitchfork suddenly sailed from the ranks of smelly steeds. The tool flew a good fifty feet through the air and found its mark, slamming dead center in the man's chest, coming out the back as if looking for earth to turn. The ganger fell backward, a bloody scream issuing from his lips. Several dozen of the Strathers bunch who had surrounded Stone now looked around terrified, wondering if they should make a run for it. But by then it was already too late. The army of mules spread out to two flanks and cut them off. Then they closed in.

It was a bloody, bloody battle as the Strathers bunch unloaded their firearms right into the charging brigade. A shitload of the farmers went down, as did many of the animals. But the farmers had already come to terms with the fact that many of them—maybe all of them—would die. And they were no longer afraid. They waded into the killers with their simple farm tools. But blades that cut grass, razor edges that slice weeds, will cut human flesh just as easily. And they tore into the Strathers ranks like they were reaping a wheatfield. The gangers fell like flies, bleeding from numerous vents. Stone fired carefully, shot after single shot, making each one count, as he was almost cleaned out of ammunition, and Excaliber took out a knee or a face here and there, dropping the bastards in their tracks.

It almost appeared to Stone that things were actually looking up when down the street, on the run, came nearly sixty more of the Strathers bunch, all carrying heavy weaponry from their armory. They came in blasting, and a dozen of the farmers fell from their mounts, splattered in red. The two groups surged together, and fierce fighting again erupted, with faces disappearing and chests opening up like umbrellas everywhere. But the farmers were now clearly getting the worst of it. And Stone, having fired his last shot, was down to using his blade in one hand, his pistol butt in the other, à la Davy Crockett's last moments at the Alamo. He heard the pitbull snarling and ripping at something, then turned to see the creature biting at the face of one of the Strathers boys. All he could see was red, and all he could hear were the screams. But it was just a holding action. Stone couldn't kid himself. The slugs were flying closer by the second.

Suddenly there was a high-pitched sound that caught every man's attention. They all looked to the right down the main street, and out of the misty air was riding a fleet of motorcycles. The Head Stompers coming full blast, their bikes roaring like a herd of stampeding elephants. It took only seconds for the attacking army to come clearly into view, and when they did, those who had been fighting in the center of the street stopped all battle for a moment to watch, so bizarre and terrifying was the sight.

There were nearly three dozen of them, and they stood atop the seats of their bikes, steering them with ropes and belts attached to the handlebars. They pulled at the things like horses' reins and drove at full speed, letting loose with a screeching war cry that would have set a corpse's skin to crawling. They moved at incredible speed, their huge, muscled bodies bare from the waist up and covered with fresh tattoos and war paint. So at ease were they atop their bikes, even at seventy or eighty miles per hour, it looked like they had been born there.

Suddenly it dawned on the Strathers gang, which was spread out along the street in mortal battle with the farmers, that perhaps the Head Stompers were after *them*. They whipped their guns around on the new threat—the farmers could wait. Most of them were wounded or half unconscious from a blow, anyway. They turned their trembling weapons and tried to sight up on the fleet of black machines that seemed to accelerate even as they approached, like jets reaching takeoff speed down a runway. The Strathers crew should have started firing sooner; for suddenly the biker leader, Bronson, unwhipped his chain from around his huge bicep and, gripping it in his right hand, began swinging it around his head. The others did the same, until there were thirty-six of the razor-sharp scythes twirling around from six to ten feet around them, whistling out a chorus of shrill sounds that made the blood drain from every one of the Strathers boys, like milk from a dead cow.

They opened up, but the bikers were already on them. Scythes swung around like guillotines, slicing right through their human targets so that arms, hands, legs, and heads flew freely through the air in a meteor shower of humanity. The farmers crawled out of the way the moment they saw the bikers closing in. They hid in the nearby alleys and among the bodies of the already dead as they watched both gangs clash in bloody battle. Stone managed to grab Excaliber, who was only too ready to leap into the fray, and pulled him behind a small pile of bodies so that they were hidden for a second.

It was war. A bloody, screaming, limb-flying war. The two gangs fought against each other with fanatical hatred. For years they had been battling one another psychologically as they tried to rip apart a town that would have been too small for just one of them. Now it all came out in an avalanche of hate and bullets and swinging scythes. It was hard to tell just what the hell was going on. The bikers rode through the ranks of the Strathers gunmen. And when they had roared past and the air had cleared for a moment, Stone could see that a good forty bodies covered the street. But a lot still remained standing. And they turned, reloading frantically to meet the bikers, who had stopped about a hundred yards past and regrouped for a second attack.

With a war scream, they closed in again, swinging their death blades, and Stone could see that they'd taken heavy losses, too—they were down to perhaps half of their original numbers. But there was no surrender here, no laying down of peace terms. They would fight until all the men on one side had been killed. The bikers again waded into the frantically firing Strathers boys, as the farmers waited on the sides of the street, occasionally taking a stray bullet or the circular cut of a scythe, sending some part of them on a quick trip off their body. It was a living bloody hell. Blade severed flesh, bullet splattered nose and heart, knife sliced liver and pancreas, chain cracked skulls and released brains like pistachio nuts from their shells.

When the dust and blood had cleared again, Stone could see that there were but two Strathers boys and one biker left. He rode past about seventy-five feet and turned. And as he turned, Stone saw that it was Bronson, shot in two places, the blood oozing out but not nearly finished. Not as long as there were ever two of the bastards left who had mutilated his son. The biker started forward, and as he drove the bike, standing up on the seat with a demonic grin and began swinging the scythe chain getting up a good speed so it would behead properly, the biker leader spotted Stone and the dog hiding behind a corpse pile. This only increased his fury and desire for revenge, and he pulled back hard on the reins of his bike, sending it flying forward like a bobsled down a mountain.

The last of the Strathers boys who were still capable of standing and firing weapons tried to get a bead on the biker, but it was impossible. He came at them like a phantom jet.

Suddenly he was just there, swinging the scythe like a madman. Two heads went shooting up into the air, crashing down to each side of the street and coming to rest against the curb like bloody bocci balls. Bronson wheeled the motorcycle around and, without stopping, came right at Stone, screaming at the top of his lungs.

"My boy, my boy, my boy."

"Oh, shit," Stone spat out as he saw that his little hill of bodies wasn't the place to hang out anymore. Suddenly he noticed it, parked in the alley alongside the brothel—his Harley. It had been moved earlier by the staff of the place, which had been hosing down outside. Son of a bitch, if he could just make it there.

"Dog, stay here, don't go after this guy. Hear me—or you're hamburger." With that, he leapt out from the body screen and tore ass across the street. But the biker was even faster than he had thought, for suddenly the man was towering over him, the screaming blade glistening like the jaws of death. Stone leapt to the side but felt the blade whiz right along his leg. A slice from thigh to knee was opened up in an instant, a half inch deep, blood soaking out through his pants and dripping into his boot.

The biker roared past, throwing the brakes on as Stone rose and rushed with all his strength toward the Harley. But the belt was missing from the front-mounted machine gun. And Bronson had already come to a stop about a hundred and fifty feet away and was starting back again. Stone could feel his leg starting to swell up from the coagulating blood in the wound. He couldn't run anymore. He was tired of running from *this* bastard, anyway. Suddenly he remembered the Luchaire 89-mm—the missile-launching system built into the side of the bike. He prayed that he'd reloaded the damn thing. And as he undid the latch that held the tube in place and swiveled it out on stainless-steel hinges, he saw that he had.

"Okay, bastard, do your best," Stone whispered under his breath as he sighted down the long tube, trying to find the man in its double-sighting system. But Bronson wasn't waiting around for anyone to get a clear fix on him. Whipping back and forth across the street by pulling the "reins" of his bike, the biker leader came at Stone atop his roaring chopper, the blade spinning faster with every turn.

"Bye bye, motherfucker." Stone grunted and pulled the trigger. There was a roar of fire right behind him as the tail of the thing shot out. Then the missile burst from the launching tube at tremendous velocity. Bronson was about sixty feet away from Stone, just looking for a good spot to sink his scythe into, when the missile hit him. It made contact right at the handlebars of the bike, sending the entire metal package up into a volcanic eruption of metal and blood and steaming flesh that continued to rain down for minutes. Stone thought he saw the head of the biker spinning wildly overhead like a satellite heading back up into orbit, and a few other parts and pieces here and there shooting off in the fiery smoke of the explosion.

Stone raised himself up on one trembling arm so he was

resting on the top of his bike. Here and there around the bloody street he could see a few of the Strathers boys and a few of the bikers still alive. Still crawling around trying to kill one another, slashing throats, strangling. Anything. It was a death trip to the end. And everybody won. Those who didn't do each other in, Stone saw, the farmers took care of. They came out of hiding with expressions of sheer pleasure, with smiles crossing their pain-stricken mouths for the first time in years. They closed in on all who were still living and made them dead.

66 "Jesus, you've brought me a lot of fucking business."
Undertaker chuckled, wiping his brow as he stood
among his coffin wagons, which were parked along
both sides of the street. His brood swarmed among the dead,
stripping them of anything of value, then sorted the bodies
by size for later coffin fitting.

"They did it to each other," Stone whispered as he looked
around at the carnage, shaking his head. "I had hoped from
the start that I could set them against each other," he said to
the coffin maker. "Play on their jealousies and fears of one
another. But it worked beyond my wildest expectations. The
suckers just blew each other away, down to the last man."

"Well, I hate to say it, but I think you've just put a severe
crimp in my coffin business," Undertaker said, looking
around at the wholesale death. "Not that there won't be more
deaths, to say the least, but nothing like it's been. Not that I
mind." He laughed. "We'll adjust, switch over to farming
more, selling junk, maybe make furniture out of all that coffin wood I got stacked up. My damn clan can do anything. It
will be wonderful to see this town filled with life the way it

once was. People with smiles instead of blood on their faces."

And even as he spoke, the townspeople, who had lived under the yokes of the two gangs for years now, came out of their various hovels and basements, came out to see what had happened to those who had beat them and raped their women, had stolen all that was valuable from them and then beat them again. These people came out of the woodwork, and they walked among those who had hurt them. And as Stone watched, they kicked out and punched at the already dead. They smacked and spat at the cleaved open skulls with rolling pins. Somehow they tried to release their anger and grief on the cooling corpses of both gangs. And perhaps it helped. For as they walked off, tears in their eyes, there was also something new. Something that hadn't been there for a long, long time: hope.

"Well, it's just fitting that we should go out of the coffin business with a bang," Undertaker said as he looked around at all the bodies being stacked like firewood. "Damn, are we going to be busy! Need any overtime work?" he asked Stone, pulling out a few silver dollars from his pocket and jangling them in front of him trying to tempt the man.

"Sorry, Undertaker, I just kill the slime—I don't bury them. It's not in the union contract." He looked around and saw Excaliber slowly walking over to him. The pitbull kept turning and licking at the gash of lion claws that had ripped all along its right side. Stone looked down at his own bleeding and battered body. He needed some R n' R bad. He thought suddenly of LuAnn, back at the Hanson place, and he looked over at Undertaker, who had a notepad in his hand and was already counting up the dead.

"Maybe I could use a little work, if I could get back that room I was staying in up in the attic. Just for a day or two."

"Stay as long as you want son, as long as you want." Undertaker laughed, slapping Stone on the back. "Any man who can bang a nail into a coffin lid is welcome in my house."

"Thanks Undertaker," Stone said softly, glancing up at an

immense cloud that blotted out the hazy sun, casting the entire town into shadow.

A razor chill ran up and down his spine. He must be going mad. The fucking cumulus looked like a woman—like April—long flowing tresses of puffy hair sprayed out around mile-wide shoulders. And as he watched, the cloud seemed to come apart, the head being suddenly severed from the rest of its cottony body by a high current of wind. The cloud head soared off trailing tendrils of ethereal white as it spun around lost in the atmosphere miles above. And Stone knew that there was no rest. Not for him. As long as April was out there—alive—his journey couldn't end. Though he wished more than anything to stay, and heal, and make sweet love to LuAnn for days at a time, when the next morning sun rose, Martin Stone would be on his way back out into hell again.